DRAGON DREAMER

J. S. Burke

LIND PRESS
Athens, Georgia

Library of Congress Control Number: 2014905532

ISBN: 978-0-9960425-0-5

Printed in the United States of America

First Edition

This is a work of fiction. Names, characters, places, and incidents either are products of the author's imagination or are used fictitiously. Any resemblance to real people, living or dead, or to actual events or places, is entirely coincidental.

Author Site: www.jennysburke.com

DEDICATION

For Roger, Lisa, and Diana

ACKNOWLEDGMENTS

Extra special thanks to Anna, who helped long before this became a book, and to Annalise. For useful insights and suggestions, thanks to Cheryl, Diana, Lisa, Roger, Carol, Sophia, Zoe, and Becky. I'm very grateful to my editors, Zee and Janice. Thank you to Lind Press. Thanks to all of you who helped in the dragon world!

How many dragons?

CONTENTS

CHAPTER 1: THE CLAW OF THE STORM

Black clouds rolled silently overhead, devouring stars in the darkening night sky. A sudden barrage of lightning crackled above. Startled by the noise, Arak spun in the air. Again the lightning flashed! In the blinding light he clearly saw the monstrous black claw of the storm. His body shook as powerful waves of thunder rolled through him. His heart beat with the new rhythm.

The young dragon veered left, toward the weaker side of a storm. But this storm was huge. There was no escape.

Thunder roared as jagged spears of lightning tore open the sky, unleashing a fierce hail of ice-stones. The stones hammered Arak's golden-scaled body as he twisted and turned, trying desperately to fly above the storm. Each wing stroke was a struggle to rise against the onslaught. The hail drove him back down, battered and bruised.

Arak sought the edge of the storm, hoping to out-fly it. But it moved like a pack of ravenous dweer, spreading rapidly to cover any escape. He realized with frightening clarity that he might never see home again. The storm raged like a living creature. He was trapped.

A swath of smaller hailstones appeared and he dove for the opening! Just as he reached the storm's edge, a huge ice-stone tore through the leathery membrane of his left wing. Air whistled through the gaping hole. Arak struggled to fly. It was like trying to breathe without lungs. Then he was beyond the grasp of the storm, falling as he flew with ragged, painful strokes.

His eyes burned from the strain as he scoured the darkness for a safe place to land. Safe? He hadn't given that a thought when he charged out to sea, abandoning his planned route, too angry to think. A distant spot of white shone faintly on the black sea. Ice!

Arak lurched through the sky, still falling, straining to reach the ice floe before he fell into the water. Then he would be trapped in the wintry sea, unable to launch from the water, his body cooling into an eternal sleep. He would die.

The frozen sky chilled his body, numbing the pain and tugging at his eyelids. No! He could not give in to sleep. But he let his eyes close, just for a moment, and rested his wings. Gliding unevenly, he drifted toward sleep. In the misty borders of dreamland, Arak saw his sire and dam watching from the dragon shore. They waited for him to return.

Arak forced his eyes open and stretched his battered wings, wincing as he reached for a stronger stroke. He pulled his gilded arms tighter against his body, streamlined to fly farther with each painful stroke of his wings. His legs and long, slender tail trailed behind.

The small sheet of ice seemed an impossible goal, as

distant as a dream. The black sea grew larger, reaching for him.

*   *   *

Time was running out. Scree gazed up through the sea with longing, her two golden eyes trying to pierce the liquid darkness above. The small octopus held her healer's bag in two tightly-coiled arms. Could she find the quithra before it was too late?

Scree looked back at the lively undersea celebration and her arms drooped. She was bound here by a promise. She smoothed her skin, keeping its natural red-brown color. Then she flowed slowly back to the pod, using her many arms to glide across the sea floor, moving as effortlessly as a shadow.

The New Moon Festival was filled with delightful entertainment. An eight-armed drummer, wielding thick sticks of coral, pounded an irresistible rhythm on giant clamshells. Scree tapped three arms in a complex pattern that matched the drumbeats pulsing through her boneless body. Anxious to leave, she restlessly poked holes in the sand.

Tempting flavors from the lavish buffet swirled around Scree, but she'd already eaten her fill of spiced crab and oysters. It was harder to ignore the huge white pearl that flashed through the water, shining like the moon, tossed and caught by a whirling octopus. She loved to dance.

Scree waited impatiently, curling her arms in frustration. Why must they always celebrate the new moon? It was tradition, but . . . couldn't they celebrate something else? Life was tied to moon cycles, and this was an important time to collect healer supplies.

She should leave now, to find the ice floe that would

attract quithra. These small, colorful creatures spawned only once a year, with the new winter moon, so she needed to gather their eggs tonight. Quithra eggs were a crucial ingredient in her potent salve for aching muscles. But she could not leave before Orm's performance.

At last, Orm pulsed onto the small stage.

He settled onto a large coral head and let his eight tentacle arms hang down. Orm put three front arms together, straight, and flattened them to enlarge the living screen of his body. Vivid pictures flashed across his body screen as he shared a pod legend. Special color cells in his skin provided realistic detail. He used another arm on either side to weave words through the water.

Tall poles were set in the sand, arranged like rings around the full moon. The top of each pole held a container of food and small glowing creatures swarmed about them, lighting the festival. Scree could see Orm clearly by this light, and the cluster of youngsters near the stage. They were unnaturally still, mesmerized by his story-telling.

Scree smiled as her mate explained that there were four New Moon Festivals every year, one for each season, to celebrate the Moon. Orm told his favorite legend: the Moon and the First Octopus. He finished with a dramatic flourish.

The entire audience erupted in silent applause.

Bright octopus arms shot up through the gray water, with skin changed from a dull brown into neon colors. Scree waved emerald arms with lines of pure gold. Other octopi chose ruby, silver, or teal. These colorful waving arms created a fantasy fountain more brilliant than a coral reef.

When the applause ended, Scree turned brown again and gripped her bag more firmly. She slipped from the rock, anxious to be on her way. Suddenly, a bright red arm snaked out and wrapped around one of her arms. She jerked away in surprise.

Orm's whole body was scarlet. "Why must you leave? This is the Winter Festival!"

Scree stroked his arm with a soothing gesture. "I need to find the quithra tonight, before they spawn." His angry color slowly faded.

Just as Scree turned to leave, her good friend Tron took the stage. He looked right at her and waved an enthusiastic welcome. With an octopus sigh she settled back again, still clutching her bag. Would she be too late?

Scree fiddled with her healer's bag. It was a gift from a grateful patient, to replace her old, tattered kelp sack. The bag was made from cloth-of-gold, woven from the thin, wiry strands of pen shells. The golden fabric was nearly indestructible. Tiny brown shells covered the gleaming cloth, giving Scree's bag a natural, earthy appearance similar to her skin. Inside were four compartments, separated by the flexible skeletons of sea fans.

The first compartment held needles, vials filled with odd liquids, medicinal seaweeds, and pearls. The second had tightly-rolled kelp bandages and live limpets. The third held empty shell containers for collecting, sponges to clean wounds, and a sharp surgeon's knife of glittering black garnet. The last held crab claws, food for her delayed journey.

Tron signaled the drummers to begin. He stretched his body tall and turned chalky white. Small spikes sprouted on his eight arms as they became stiff, jointed legs. His head broadened to mimic the lumpy-flat shell of a northern king crab.

Tron began the dance of this huge crab. Four of his legs tapped one rhythm while the legs in-between tapped another. The drumming grew faster and he quickened the pace. The beat stopped. He smoothed his skin and flowed back to his normal red-brown, flexible shape.

Scree waved her arms high, turning them bright colors to show appreciation. Tron's performance was remarkable. Octopi were natural shape-shifters, able to change their shape, color and texture to mimic many different creatures. But few learned the dances of others.

Tron was a rare friend, since only he and Scree explored alone. He knew the feel of cold snow brushing your skin, the taste of melting ice, and the rapture of colored lights waving like seaweed in the night sky. Would Orm ever experience this?

Scree turned to her mate. "I must leave now, but I'll be back soon."

"Please be careful." Orm's arms curled and uncurled with anxiety. "It's not safe to be alone, away from the pod."

Scree sighed. It *was* unnatural to travel alone. Most octopi appreciated the security of a village, with its seafood farms and sturdy dens. Each spring, many thousands of octopus eggs hatched. The tiny hatchlings drifted far from home on sea currents. Few survived.

Orm was a young juvenile on the return migration when a shark tore by and killed all of his comrades. Scree still saw the haunting memory in his eyes. He could not believe that anything she found was worth the terrible risk of exploring. Scree twined two arms affectionately with her mate. "Your research can be done here, but I must leave to gather healing supplies."

Orm handed her a large pearl. "For luck."

6

"A black pearl . . . that's new. It's beautiful." She placed it in her bag and looked into his eyes. "I will be careful." Scree flowed away into the darkness.

Scree pulsed through the inky dark waters toward the starlit surface, seeking rare items for her healer's bag. She also sought solitude and the magic of the stars, which shone in their full glory during the new moon. Few octopi ventured so far from home. Fewer still risked the dangers of a journey through open water, with no place to hide.

Scree twirled beneath the starry sky. Then she headed for a small ice floe that she'd found earlier, where a weathered branch protruded. The branch was a rare, desirable perch, likely to attract quithra.

Quithra were lovely sea slugs with long oval bodies of brilliant violet and rose. A dozen fleshy yellow spikes ran down the back, and each spike ended in a blue eye dot that could see only light and dark. They sought the surface when it was time to spawn, releasing their eggs. Like many slow, vivid creatures, quithra were poisonous to eat. Their bright color served as a warning. The oily eggs tasted bitter, were slightly toxic, and had a numbing effect that was perfect for her salve.

Scree twined an arm around the branch, looking. There were no quithra. Was she too late? She shivered as eddies of fog from the ice blew in cold swirls across her skin. She gathered a cluster of red seaweed, useful for dressing wounds, and stowed it in her healer's bag. Then she waited, nervously changing colors, hoping for quithra.

Scree felt a slight change in the currents. What was it? She turned to stone, not moving, while her eyes searched the sea. Quithra! Three swam slowly toward her, using their muscular body flaps. They settled on the branch and began to spawn. Scree eagerly collected clouds of small, bright yellow eggs on her sponge. She placed the sponge securely inside a clam shell purse and added it to her bag.

A golden streak seared the dark sky. A falling star! Her eyes widened as it plunged toward the small ice sheet, growing to the size of a shark. The crash shattered the night, rocking the ice and almost knocking her off her log seat. The star flopped, in a very un-starlike manner.

Scree had never seen anything like it.

She instantly camouflaged, changing her color to match the log perfectly. Scree could stretch about two feet across between the tips of her arms. But this frightful, alien creature must be at least eight feet long and it had gleaming sharp claws. She trembled and flowed away, matching the log as she moved, invisible.

Scree glanced back, ready to slip into the sea, hanging by the tip of one arm.

The creature writhed.

Scree stopped. It looked more dangerous than a shark, but it must have been injured in such an incredible fall. She felt the weight of her healer's bag, and the responsibility. She struggled to look beyond the deadly claws, noticing instead the crimson splashes of blood that stained the snow. Scree rippled back onto the branch.

* * *

The young dragon gasped for breath, stunned by the crash. Red-hot fire shot through his right leg. Arak struggled upright despite the searing pain, flinching as he tried to stand. He collapsed, twisting as he fell, writhing in agony.

"My first solo journey," he moaned.

He had reached the ice floe. But this was not the island

8

he'd hoped to discover. Dragons needed copper supplements to survive and their mine was almost empty. Finding an island source would make him a hero. The other dragons wouldn't taunt him anymore. Instead, his wing was torn and now he'd broken his leg.

Arak hung his head. Karoon was right, he was just a dreamer. He hadn't even noticed the storm signs, and he had crashed on his important first solo. He would never live this down.

The pain was growing like flames and he desperately needed help. Arak automatically reached for his chest pouch. It was gone! The ice sheet was small; it could only hold a few dragons. He looked under his wings. Nothing! His eyes frantically swept the ice, probing every thin shadow. The barren ice gleamed serenely white under the stars. Empty. There was no sign of his pouch or anything else.

Arak trembled, shaking like the last leaf on a winter tree. He had lost everything in the storm. His missing pouch held a meal, a silver flask of spiced tea, vials of rare ground metals, a magnetic lodestone, and his precious aquamarine globe . . . his trance-stone. He needed his trance-stone to contact the clan for help.

Arak was chilled to the bone. He yearned for his own cozy shelter, which was well-stocked with blankets and hearty dragon-snacks. But he was trapped on the ice, wounded and unable to fly, with no food or warmth or healer. So he would die here, alone. A sob caught in his throat. Arak watched the sea, sparkling with reflected stars, and tried to calm his mind.

* * *

Still camouflaged, Scree studied the fearsome creature

9

from the edge of the ice. It had sharp-tipped arms and a head full of sharp teeth. Only the long, slender tail seemed harmless. Unlike her eight matching arms, it had three distinctly different pairs of limbs. The huge golden fins seemed to be adapted for sky-swimming. One leg was bent at an odd angle, probably broken in the fall.

Scree knew several techniques for treating broken bones, despite the fact that she was boneless. Some of her earliest patients had been fish. But she didn't know how to communicate with this strange creature. How could she get its permission to help? And what did it eat? Hopefully not octopus! She shuddered at the thought.

Scree studied the being. It needed help, she was a healer, and she must get its attention. She took the large black pearl from her bag and rolled it to the creature's claws. The pearl gleamed like a dark rainbow against the cold white snow.

The golden head turned, following the pearl's path back to her. Its eyes grew wide.

Scree made the sign of a healer, bending her two front arms together into an upright triangle. This symbolized a broad, stable base of healer knowledge supporting the healing point of change.

There was no response.

Scree curled her arms in frustration. Then she stretched taller and concentrated on the color cells in her skin. She made a detailed picture on her body of the creature holding out its injured leg and sky-fin.

The creature stared. Then it slowly copied her picture, and a trembling sky-fin unfolded.

She was right. These injuries needed serious attention. Scree extended an arm and curled it back to herself. The creature hobbled toward her, to the edge of the ice. At least it understood that gesture!

Scree lost her fear as she became absorbed in her work. It held quite still while she bandaged the jagged tear in its wing, using sturdy kelp leaves held in place by limpets. These small sea snails with shell hats would hold tenaciously to any spot for a day. Then they'd be released and replaced with fresh limpets.

The creature watched with obvious interest but moved only as directed.

Scree felt the rough break in its leg beneath the torn scales. She cut two sturdy splints and a generous supply of gray-green kelp bandages. Then four of her rubbery arms worked together, setting and wrapping the broken bone. Her remaining four arms were spread wide for support. She added pieces of iodine-rich seaweed to protect the wound from infection.

Scree's eight flexible arms had additional brains to control the endless possible movements. They were tactile marvels lined with powerful, yet delicately sensitive, suckers. And each sucker had millions of sensory cells. As Scree dressed the wound she felt the shape and texture of the break, sensed micro-changes in temperature and tasted the salty-metallic injury. She gathered detailed information to better treat her unusual patient.

Scree sighed. Would she ever know enough? Breaks and tears were obvious problems. But with such a fall, it could have a more serious, hidden injury. Even fatal.

Scree admired the hard, diamond-shaped scales as she worked. Each scale was a golden gem tipped with ruby-red, covering its body in a perfect mosaic. A ridge of sharp gold scales ran down the back of its long, slender neck.

She checked the leg wrap once more, making sure it was neither too tight nor too loose. Then she knotted the bandage and trimmed it above the splints. Finished, she flowed back to rest on the submerged half of the log, with her head above the water.

Scree and the sky-being studied each other. Its big, aqua-blue eyes looked remarkably like Orm's, brimming with curiosity; she could almost see the myriad questions sparkling within. Only the color was different. Such familiar eyes in a strange creature seemed stranger still.

The alien bowed its head, seeming grateful.

Scree bobbed her head in return, wondering what that really meant. Was it hungry? She mimed eating, raising an arm repeatedly to her mouth.

The sky-being copied her mime and added a vigorous nod.

Scree slipped an arm into her bag and tossed the crab claws up onto the ice, one by one. Each claw landed neatly at its feet with a thunk and a spray of ice. Then she slumped back, arms hanging limp. Her skin was tinged gray with exhaustion. Her stomach was an empty cave, and she had just given the patient her entire supply of journey food.

She watched warily as it crunched through the hard shells. Long, fearsome claws extracted every last shred of meat. Then it raked through the remains, wrinkling its nose, searching hungrily. Her patient clearly needed more food. It would also need bedding against the cold ice, since she had felt warmth beneath her arms while wrapping its leg. A potion made with crushed coral would help the bones grow together. And . . .

Scree made a mental list of supplies, hoping she had enough strength to gather everything. Weary and weak with hunger, she mimed leaving and returning. Did it understand?

It gazed steadily back, a sharp-edged alien, deadly and helpless. Scree grasped her healer's bag and slid off the log. The glow of its eyes reached through the darkness, watching her as she sank into the sea.

Was there a hidden injury? Would her patient be alive when she returned?

CHAPTER 2: SILVER LINING

A wave of loneliness washed over Arak when the creature disappeared into the sea. He nervously rolled the shimmering black gem from claw to claw. What *was* that strange, floppy creature, with no bones or scales? Why had it helped? His stomach growled. Would it return? Too hungry and restless to sleep, he relived his disastrous journey. His first solo journey.

The glorious Winter Festival had just ended, with dragon games and a bounteous feast. Arak took the final test for his journey. He passed easily, surprising the elders with the strength of his trance-mind. The thoughts he shared mind-to-mind were crystal clear.

Arak remembered the frozen sand crunching beneath his claws as he stood on the shore, impatiently waiting to leave. Most dragons journeyed during the summer, but he just couldn't wait for his solo. He planned to fly south along the coast, looking for copper, of course.

He fidgeted as the clan leader droned on and on, giving him final instructions. Arak was so eager to explore that he barely listened. He knew what to do.

His sire and dam stood proudly by, and his friend Taron. The other young dragons who came to watch were probably just curious about Dreamer, the trance-freak.

Zarina landed and waved a friendly greeting, zigging her claws in a jagged lightning path to wish him well. Then Karoon appeared and made a joke about Arak's safe, predictable journey course.

Karoon stretched a wing toward Zarina, laughing.

That did it! Arak launched skyward and headed west, winging out to sea. He ignored the commands of the leader and the worried look of his parents. He knew the dangers. But this winter had been mild, with few storms. The clan barely had enough snow for their festival.

He tore through the sky, flying above the vast sea.

When the dragon shore disappeared, sea and sky met in a perfect circle. As he flew, Arak remained in the center; the circle moved with him. He was alone in a private world. There was no fixed shore to judge the distance he'd flown, and no trees with lengthening shadows to mark the march of time.

Above an endless sea, beyond the touch of time, Arak flew further and further from home.

Arak looked down, searching the sea as he flew, determined to find a copper-filled island. That would impress the clan. He looked up and snapped his tail nervously. The sun was low in the sky. How far had he flown?

He should have turned back long ago.

Then the gray-green sea exploded with color. The spectacular sunset was a parade of rainbow sky colors mirrored in a canvas of curved water scales. As the red sun melted into the sea, Arak wondered if he could capture this display in an ice sculpture. The idea grew in his mind as a storm spread silently far overhead.

Totally absorbed, Arak missed the subtle shifts in

temperature and pressure that herald an ice storm. Dreamer! Dragons ridiculed him for tuning out the world, lost in thought or trance. Nothing good could come of it. Arak sighed. Maybe they were right. It was particularly humiliating to be injured by a storm. Dragons knew storms. They danced with storms! Yet he'd missed the signs, and this one almost killed him.

Arak shivered and curled into a ball, trying to get warm. He tucked his head beneath his wing and closed his weary eyes. His mind replayed a familiar legend.

The First Dragon was born of Storm, made from the four elements of life: Fire, Water, Air, and Land. Ruby lightning blazed through the rain-drenched sky and struck the golden sand. A golden dragon-lord leapt out of the smoking crater, with bright scales edged in red. He flew as fast as the gray winds and breathed storm-fire. He danced with lightning to honor the Storm.

But the dragon-lord was lonely. So the Storm used a rare shaft of emerald lightning, the color of new spring leaves, to create a dragon-lady with gold scales edged in green. The dragons spiraled up together into the clouds and flew with the Storm.

Arak opened his eyes to the starlit sky. He had been careless, but he would never have met such an intriguing being if he hadn't crashed. The silver lining in his dark cloud of problems was so bright it was incandescent.

Pain and hunger grew as the night wore on. Arak rocked back and forth, trying to distract himself with the rhythm. Pain, Hunger, Exhaustion, and Cold: the new four elements of life, he thought, in a feeble attempt at dragon humor.

Arak stopped rocking and stared in disbelief.

A huge sea turtle swam toward the ice, towing a long stalk of kelp. And there was the healer! Deep scratches along the turtle's side gleamed silver. How odd. Part of the turtle's shell was made from sections of large abalone shells. The turtle must have been badly injured, and the sea-being fixed it. The sturdy shell pieces fitted perfectly, held together by barnacles. This healer must be skilled.

The sea-being cut the kelp into sections and pushed them onto the ice.

Arak arranged the stalks and sank onto his thick bed, propping his injured leg onto extra leaves. The earthy smell of kelp brought a comfort of home. Crab claws and red seaweed landed beside him. How did it know what he needed?

He attacked the claws and then ate the seaweed, relaxing as the furry red snack began to numb his many pains. Gentle waves lapped against his ice floe with the muffled drumbeat of a dragon's lullaby. He closed his eyes and immediately sank into a deep sleep.

* * *

The water lightened around Orm, bringing to life a seascape of jewel-toned plants and animals. Small copper fish darted through a forest of coral branches. Bright orange starfish hunted along the reef, stalking clams hidden beneath the sand.

Orm fed plankton to his carefully bred bioluminescent tunicates. These small, clear, jelly-like animals glowed in colors, and they could be attached to any surface by holding their base against it. The walls of the entrance chamber in Orm's cave were covered with tunicates. His elegant, living mosaic glowed in vibrant reds, blues and greens.

Orm headed for his shellfish farm. He flowed past Scree's cave and peered in. Empty. Where was she? He flexed his many arms with restless energy. Frilly red worms, sensitive to the slightest movement, vanished into their holes in the coral. He turned in a circle, gazing into the distance. Then he looked up through the sea. Where was Scree?

Orm continued on to the farm and checked the many oyster beds, calming himself with work. The oysters were healthy and growing well; they would feed the pod. Next he checked the three small groups of oysters that were fed special diets. He'd finally found a way to grow colored pearls. One experimental group had produced a few rare, black pearls. He checked another group and his arms curled in distress. These oysters were dying. Why?

Puzzling the problem, Orm moved on to his abalone crop. He removed a few brightly colored pearls and smiled. He'd just succeeded in growing these exotic, organic opals. The shimmering pearls had interwoven layers of color. The pink-gold and blue-green balls were particularly stunning.

Orm continued his work, often checking the seas above, searching for Scree.

* * *

Scree drifted down through the sea, too exhausted to pulse. She sank limply to the sand and collapsed in her cave, dead to the world. Watery blue-green shadows lengthened into evening. She opened her eyes just as Orm poked his head into her cave.

"You've slept all day. Where were you?"

Twining arms, Scree drew him in. "You won't believe this."

"Try me." Orm handed Scree a large clam shell filled

18

with succulent oysters and colorful sprigs of seaweed. "But first, let's eat."

They feasted together while Orm glanced around at Scree's cave, eyeing the shelves. There were rolls of kelp bandages and a bowl filled with live limpets. Shell containers held sedative poisons, seaweed drugs, special salves and supplements. A bright red box carved from coral had sharp, hollow needles. These were made of spines from the fin of a dead lion-fish. In life, the beautiful fish could inject deadly poison through its fin.

Then Scree told her story.

Orm flushed gold in response to Scree's body-picture of the strange, golden creature. His arms danced with interest. "Where did it come from? What crops do these creatures grow? What art do they make?"

"I think it lives far to the east, on the shore. We're still learning to communicate. This being is so different from us but, when I look into its eyes, they look like yours. Only the color is different. I can almost see it thinking." Scree laughed. "When we can talk properly, I believe it will ask as many questions as you do!"

"You found a good use for that black pearl. I'd like to meet this creature. I'm in the middle of experiments and I'm having problems, but I should be finished before the full moon."

Scree frowned. "Those shellfish farms are important to the pod. I love this food, and your pearls are a beautiful bonus. What's wrong?"

"I'm experimenting with oyster diet, using trace metals. Some oysters are growing like seaweed, and I've learned how to change the color of their pearls. But one group is dying and I need to know why."

"Metals can be tricky. This sky-being should be healed and gone before you finish your work." Scree paused, considering. "I think it may visit again," she added.

"We should tell Spar. He *is* the pod leader."

Scree's arms went rigid and her skin flushed with colors. "I'm not ready to tell him. He didn't support my healing a stingray, even though it's a fish! And this is an alien creature. He might not approve, but it doesn't matter. I'm a healer!"

"Spar lost the use of an arm to that stingray," Orm said.

Scree glared angrily. "I had everything under control! The fish panicked because Spar interfered and scared it."

Orm sighed. "Very well, I'll say nothing. But Spar might need to know. Eventually, you should tell him."

Scree's arms relaxed back to normal. "I know. Orm, the meal was wonderful."

"Someone needs to make sure that you eat."

Scree just smiled. He knew her so well! Orm was her mate and long-time companion. They mated once each year and carefully tended the eggs for a moon cycle until they hatched. Scree and Orm took turns gently stroking the hanging egg curtain, careful to oxygenate all the eggs with new seawater. There were many hundreds of eggs, but few hatchlings would survive their season of drifting on the surface. Any that grew into juveniles and migrated home would be welcomed back to the pod.

Scree glanced at Orm. Had any of their offspring survived? She would never know.

Scree grabbed seaweed samples and stuffed them into her healer bag. "Crabs alone can't properly nourish this sky-being. It has golden scales and copper claws, so it probably needs special trace metals." She added a chunk of turquoise for its copper content, a clamshell for mixing, and a small sack of crushed coral.

Scree twined arms affectionately with Orm and left, heading back to her patient.

*　　*　　*

Three dragon-weeks had passed, Arak's wounds were healed, and it was time to leave. The dawn sky flushed with gold and rose as the sun climbed above the sea. Colors caught on the waves and brushed the clouds, surrounding his ice floe with deceptive warmth.

Arak grinned joyfully at Scree as he fastened the new kelp pouch securely across his chest. He inhaled the aroma of raw oysters and seaweed from the meal inside. Then he flamed a hollow of ice and collected water in his carved coral flask. The pouch, food and flask were gifts from Scree for his long flight home.

Arak was ready to leave, but it was surprisingly hard to say good-bye. "How do you make skin pictures?" he asked, instead. They communicated well now, using snow pictures, mimes, and Scree's body pictures.

Scree's entire body suddenly turned bright green, then blue, then pink, like an exotic flower. Arak snapped his tail up and down in amazement.

"There are many color cells in my skin, and cells that are almost like eyes. When I feel danger, I change colors to match my background." Scree camouflaged, perfectly matching her log seat, and then changed back to her normal red-brown. "We learn to control this ability, to make an image of choice." A detailed, golden picture of Arak emerged from her skin.

Scree pointed to his wing. "How was it hurt?"

21

Arak slashed his claws like rain and lifted an ice ball. "Storm ice tore it."

Scree nodded. "A storm pearl."

Arak shrugged his wings. They were the same shape, and storm pearl was a good octopus name for an ice ball.

"Orm is interested in dragon art," she said.

"Kragor would love to talk with him! Our Winter Festival is full of art. Winter storms drive us into the cave, and crowding can lead to fights. Art is good way to channel all that edgy energy."

Arak stretched his claws to frame a circle larger than Scree's head. "Dragon-ladies grow big snowflakes in the clouds. Most have patterns with animals." He sketched an ornate, six-pointed design into the smooth-packed snow using a sharp copper claw.

Scree peered at the drawing. "Fish and sea grass," she said approvingly.

"Dragon-lords carve ice sculptures with facets that bend the light. This makes glowing pictures inside the ice that change with time." It would be so much easier to describe if he could make skin pictures as Scree did.

Scree tilted her head in a dragon-like gesture. "I'd like to see them. Orm works with a different type of cold light. He breeds tiny creatures that glow and uses them to make living murals." Scree imaged the colorful walls of Orm's alcove. "He wants to meet you."

Arak studied the beautiful, alien artwork. "Let's meet here again."

"The next full moon would be a good time to visit." Scree pointed to the floe and slowly moved her arm southwest. "The ice is drifting southwest and will be closer to my village when you return." Reaching up, she twined an arm around Arak's claws. "My falling star is ready to rejoin the heavens. I'll miss you, my friend."

Arak reached for another arm, for the double clasp of friendship. He would truly miss Scree, with her easy acceptance and fascinating perspectives. She was, unexpectedly, a kindred spirit.

Morning mist rose off the ice like steam from a scalding-hot mug of tea. Tonight he would enjoy the spicy flavors of that dragon drink. Arak wanted the familiar crunch of sand under his claws, the traditional aroma of roasting fish, and the freedom of wind beneath his wings. He wanted the liveliness of the clan.

Taron was his best friend, like a nest-mate. Zarina listened to him, but she'd grown and now he felt awkward with her. Arak even missed his parents, despite the irritating way that they fussed over him. Why did they worry so much? He did not miss Karoon.

It would be good to see home again, though he could only imagine the painful jokes about crashing. But he'd been teased as long as he could remember. Karoon made it his mission to point out Arak's odd behavior. Sometimes, lost in thought or trance-mind, Arak completely missed a meal, unheard of for a dragon! How could you depend on a dragon so lost to the world?

Arak stretched his wings, loosening the muscles, and tried to shake away these memories. If he'd found copper, all would be forgiven. Instead, he'd found Scree. He didn't think the clan would be able to see her value.

Arak reached into his pouch and handed the lustrous black pearl to Scree. "It's a beautiful gem."

She signed her refusal. "It is a gift."

"It's a great treasure." Arak bowed his thanks and leapt

into the sky.

At last! He swooped low over the water, recklessly brushing the waves with the tips of his claws. Cool wind rushed by as he soared into the sky and playfully executed a loop before leveling off. He circled once in farewell before heading for home. His ice floe became a mere speck and then disappeared from sight.

It would be a long flight over the sea, with no place to rest. But his torn wing had healed and Arak was sure he could reach the dragon shore.

CHAPTER 3: THE BLACK PEARL

Arak reached the dragon shore as evening colors drained from the sky. He collapsed onto the beach at the water's edge. Winter waves crashed over him and rolled back, dragging his limp body into the sea.

He struggled upright and staggered up the beach, digging his clawed feet into the cold, gritty sand. The wet sand gleamed like copper in the sunset. Solid land. He was home!

Arak savored the lingering aroma of char-grilled fish. The clan gathered every evening at the long stone table, where each dragon brought something to share. It was a mark of honor to bring a large fish or a well-spiced dish. After Scree's bland seafood, Arak could almost taste the potent dragon spices.

Suddenly, his parents landed on either side. Had they been watching for him? He was buried in wings, enveloped in an endless hug. Arafine's claws gripped his own hesitantly, as if he might melt away like sea mist.

"I'm all right," he reassured his dam once again.

Then the clan surrounded him.

Taron clipped his shoulder in a friendly, dragonly way, eyes glowing with relief. "Took your time, didn't you?"

Arak grinned. "Why hurry?"

"Dreamer's back," a young dragon shouted.

Arak automatically ignored this insult, focusing instead on Zarina. She watched quietly from the edge of the rowdy crowd. But they'd been friends forever! Why didn't she just wing-buffet him, as usual? Her golden scales were edged in a particularly lovely shade of blue-green. Had they always been that color? He returned her smile, wondering what had changed.

Arak grimaced as Driana, the clan healer, worked her way through the crowd toward him. A public examination of his injuries would be the spicing on the fish! Completely humiliated, Arak held out his wing for inspection. Driana carefully felt the mended edges of the tear and looked questioningly at Arak. He quietly answered, "My wing was torn by an ice-stone."

She tested the strength of his leg and gave a satisfied nod. "These have mended well. I'd like to meet your healer."

Karoon was listening, wearing the surly expression that he reserved for Arak. What new insults was he crafting? As Arak edged away from the group, Karoon almost knocked him down. He staggered off-balance from the shoulder charge, stumbling as he instinctively protected his newly-healed leg.

"Clumsy, as always," laughed Karoon, "and too slow. Couldn't escape the deadly ice predator?"

Arak smiled through gritted teeth, determined to remain calm. "Perhaps. But a faster dragon would have missed the adventure."

"Where were you?" a dragon shouted, following Arak as he tried to retreat.

"What happened?" yelled another, bringing the noisy crowd with him.

Why must everyone speak at once? Arak had forgotten the exuberance of dragons. He looked out to sea, remembering the solitude of his ice floe. Each evening, Arak and Scree shared a silent language of gestures and pictures. The sea was his quiet companion by day.

He lived with the smell and taste of sea spray, the rhythmic sound of waves, and the remarkable colors. Sunrise waves were purple and rose. Afternoon waves shimmered like hammered gold in the slanting sunlight. Sometimes the sea sparkled like a field strewn with cut diamonds. Arak wanted to leap into the sky and return to his distant refuge.

"Arak."

He looked up. Arafine, his dam, handed him a large ceramic bowl. It was filled with tempting food left over from the evening communal meal. Dragon food! Arak reached in for a piece of charred fish and stopped in his tracks. The beautiful bowl was spun from blue clay with silver threads. Moonstones and aquamarines decorated the sides in a swirly pattern, like waves of the sea.

This was Arak's nest-bowl.

But it should only be used for special occasions. What was special? He looked into Arafine's eyes and saw that they were bright with unshed tears. She must have been really worried that he would not return. "Thank you," he said, unable to put his deeper thoughts into words.

Arak flicked his tail in dismay when he noticed a cloud of steam. Soon, the rich smell of tea steeped with cinnamon bark filled the air. Each dragon brought a large ceramic mug to the fire. It was a tea ceremony to welcome him home.

When a dragon first entered trance-mind, the clan held a tea ceremony and the youngster received a special mug inlaid with his or her trance stone. Arak's mug was a swirly blue-green set with an aquamarine gem. He bowed politely as his mug was filled first. Then he stood by the fire.

A cluster of young dragons stared at him, laughing.

This was really a tea trial, not a ceremony. Why did there have to be a celebration? Now everyone would remember his crash! At least he had something truly unexpected to share. Maybe that would distract them. After the tea, Arak stood within rings of dragons to share his journey tale.

"How'd you manage to crash on your first solo?" Karoon sneered. "Were you lost in dreams, or just lost?"

Laughter sparked around the circles.

Arak cringed inside, but he'd expected this insult. "Well, I did find my way home. And I found a new world, which is like finding a dream."

He talked about Scree and the undersea village. "She makes pictures on her skin that look real, just by thinking. And Orm grows undersea crops of food."

The dragons shrugged their wings; this was difficult to imagine.

Zarina raised her wings. "How do you sign 'thank you' to an octopus?"

Arak smiled gratefully and demonstrated the simple bow. "To bid farewell, the octopus wraps the end of an arm around your claws."

"Could you show us what it looks like?" Taron asked.

Arak melt-carved an octopus from a clear block of ice; the curling arms gleamed like crystal. This captured her essence but not the complex colors.

Kragor, his sire, nodded approvingly. "Well done. You said they make art?"

"Orm covered the walls inside his cave with glowing patterns. He uses tiny animals that don't move and glow in colors."

Arak reached into his pouch and drew out the black pearl. It shimmered in the firelight with a captivating, iridescent luster. It was unlike any dragon gem. Dragons crowded around, golden tails snapping up and down like whips.

Zarina gasped. "It looks like the shadow of a new moon! This would be perfect for our festival. Where did they mine it?"

"Orm grows pearls in a special crop, but few are black."

Karana, the clan leader, asked: "Would they trade?"

Arak thumped his tail with excitement. He had not considered this possibility! Trade would redeem his failed solo journey. He straightened his wings into crisp folds.

"Scree's very interested in other beings. We plan to meet again at the ice floe." His tail slumped to the ground. "But Scree is the only octopus I met, and she's not the pod leader." Had she mentioned some disagreements with her leader? Well, it would still be good to see Scree again.

CHAPTER 4: THE SHARK

Scree playfully flicked water drops onto Orm. "Isn't the sky beautiful?" she asked. They were perched on the log that was stuck in Arak's ice floe, waiting for him to arrive.

Orm shivered as the drops ran down his skin. "It's interesting. But our reef has more color, and you don't need to travel to the surface through open water. I felt completely exposed, like shark bait," he declared.

Scree gazed into the distance, scanning the sky. Three specks appeared and slowly grew into golden shapes. She scooted up the branch at the edge of Arak's ice floe. "Wait 'til you see dragon scales. That's worth the trip!"

Orm followed her gaze. "Three? You said there'd be one." He curled his arms nervously.

A flurry of huge wings filled the air as the fearsome trio landed. Each was easily five times their size. Scree and Orm suctioned to the branch while wind buffeted their bodies. The dragons slipped on the melting ice, comically ruining their fierce façade.

Arak spun about, his claws scrabbling for traction. He plowed into a pile of slushy snow. He shook his body, wriggling like a dancing sea slug, and sprays of cold white frosting flew off.

Orm shook with silent laughter. His eyes grew wide when the dragons stopped sliding, giving him his first clear view. One had golden scales edged in emerald green, while the other two were gold with ruby. "What exquisite artwork! Your descriptions didn't do them justice."

"I knew you'd appreciate their scales," Scree said smugly.

Introductions were made, with Scree and Arak interpreting. Their sign language used dragon and octopus gestures, snow drawings and skin pictures.

Arafine bowed her head to Scree. "Thank you for saving our son."

Scree nodded in return. "I'm a healer. It was my pleasure to help."

Arafine opened her sack and displayed their gifts: various nuts, tea leaves and gemstones.

Scree made a show of handling each item. She nibbled the nuts, smiling at the subtle flavors. She felt the tea, which looked like dried seaweed but had an oddly sweet flavor. She slid an arm through the small pile of cold stones, recognizing garnet and turquoise. "What's this?" she asked, lifting a small, cloudy-clear, blue-green sphere.

"Aquamarine, the sea-gem," Arafine replied. "It's Arak's trance-stone, which seems rather fitting now."

Arak handed Scree a clear, lumpy glass rod. "I chose this because you love the sky."

31

Scree's eyes glowed. She ran her arms along the surface and peered through the solid, magically transparent shaft. "This would be perfect in the entrance to my cave! What is it? Where's it found? Are there more?"

Arak laughed with pleasure. "I knew you'd like it! This is a lightning cast. Lightning from the sky melted a path of glass through the sand. We can make more. It's a bit risky, but fun. We fly a storm and channel lightning onto beach sand, then harvest the crystal copy of its path."

Scree offered her gifts of seaweed, oysters and pearls.

Arafine and Kragor stood stock-still, mesmerized by the ocean gems. There were creamy pearls, colorful abalone pearls, and another rare black pearl. Arafine lifted a handful of pearls, eyes aglow as they slipped silkily through her claws. The lustrous gemstones were made of fine crystals that broke the light into subtle, watery rainbows.

As they shared a meal, Scree asked, "How are your healers trained?"

Arafine told of long apprenticeships and skills in manipulating crystal growth, or bone re-growth. She glanced quizzically at the small, barren ice, then at Scree. "What brought you to this ice floe?"

"I was seeking quithra eggs to make a salve when Arak landed here." Scree flashed a picture of the brightly-colored creature. "My mentor was old when she chose me, and her arms often ache. I rub in the salve to ease her pain."

Orm watched expectantly as Arak translated his question, "Do dragons face any dangers like sharks?"

Kragor nodded. "Dweer are smaller than us, but vicious. A pack of dweer can kill a dragon. But our real danger is running out of copper. We must find more, or all dragons will become deathly sick."

Orm frowned, as if seeing this future. "I grow undersea crops and I've studied metals. Seaweed can concentrate metals. I'll look for one with extra copper."

Arak translated and expressed Kragor's gratitude.

"How do dragons make fire?" Orm asked.

Kragor ignited a stream of brilliant fire, melting a swath of ice.

Orm's entire body flashed bright yellow-orange, mirroring the flames, as he was shocked into losing control of his color cells. He shuddered as a wave of heat washed over him. Orm struggled to regain his composure. Orange sparks dissolved back into his skin and he reverted to a mottled red-brown, his normal, inconspicuous coloring.

"I've never seen liquid sun. And you produce electricity like an eel!" Orm stretched out an arm, reaching through the pool of warm water that Kragor had melted. The tip of his arm slid on the slick ice below.

"I've never seen an octopus sun," Kragor replied, laughing. "And you make colors like nothing I've *ever* seen!"

Kragor explained that dragons have two stomachs. During the first two years, all food goes to the first stomach and is used for rapid growth. Dragons eat oil-rich plants and fish. When their growth slows, extra oil is stored in the second stomach, along with excess carbon. To breathe fire, a dragon spits the carbon-oil mix and ignites it with sparks from a copper claw.

Then Kragor sketched a picture in the dusting of snow. "A giant with long arms washed up on the beach. It was huge, as big as five dragons. What do you know of its kind?"

Orm made a detailed squid picture against black skin. "Giant squid live in the depths, in darkness. There's a legend that they once attacked us."

Scree smiled, amused that her careful, conservative mate was lost in conversation with a large, dangerous alien. Kragor was another Orm in dragon-form. They were both full of questions, talking non-stop. Who knew they'd have so much in common?

Their meal finished, Arafine raised her wings, commanding attention. "We would love to use that flavorful red seaweed for snow pudding, and your black pearls would be perfect for our New Moon Festival. The clan would like to trade."

Scree straightened her many arms, automatically assuming a more formal stance. "I think the pod would trade." She stiffened with concern. "But your leader should meet with ours."

Now she really would have to speak with Spar and he would not be pleased. The pod leader was predictably conservative, and did not approve of her working with dangerous creatures. He still blamed her for that stingray incident. Granted, the sharp barb must have been painful when it slashed through his arm. But it was Spar's fault for not trusting her, and he had completely recovered from the injury.

Would Spar agree to meet with them? Scree looked up at the huge dragons, trying to see them as Spar would. They were monsters, and each sharp-tipped arm had more barbs than a stingray. Would Spar be able to see past their deadly claws and appreciate the golden opportunities?

Scree ran an arm over the glass lightning cast, feeling a deep hunger. She wanted more of these sturdy, transparent rods that virtually disappeared in water. They could be installed across the entrance to an octopus cave, to protect the precious egg curtain. Octopi could squeeze their fluid, boneless bodies through the glass bars, but few predators could follow. This "glass window" would be the perfect cross between a picture window and a predator screen. It would give Scree a secure, yet perfectly clear, view of her realm.

"Spar and our leader, Karana, should meet here before this ice melts," Arafine said. "We'll leave a lodestone to help us find you, and bring a wood platform when we return."

Scree exchanged farewells with the new tradition, twining octopus arm to dragon claw. Nervously, she prepared to ask the pod leader to meet the dragons.

* * *

One moon passed. Spar, the leader, flatly rejected Scree's request to meet dragons. Then Orm convinced him to come.

Scree bobbed at the surface near the ragged, melting remains of Arak's ice floe. It had drifted right over their village. Orm, Stur, and Spar waited beside her. Spar scowled at Scree, flexing his once-injured arm. She winced and looked away.

Four pairs of wings beat against the cool night sky, gleaming gold in the light of the full moon. The dragons flew in formation, towing a large raft that bounced on the waves. They reached the ice, released the ropes and landed.

Scree helped anchor the raft to undersea boulders. Then she flowed onto one of the comfortable log seats that protruded beneath the raft.

Spar and Karana greeted each other formally, as

leaders. Then he met Arak, Kragor and Arafine.

"The clan is grateful to Scree for helping Arak," Karana said. "She's a skilled healer."

"Scree is talented," Spar replied grudgingly. His eyes moved from one hand to the next, and he seemed to be counting the sharp claws.

Karana presented Spar with two lightning casts and a container of red-root tea. "We would like to trade with your pod."

Scree watched nervously as Spar felt the clear rods and then hefted them, as if weighing their obvious value against the hazards of trade. He ran an arm across the tea, tasting the earthy-delicate flavors. He frowned and smiled at the same time, a decidedly odd expression. Scree could almost read his thoughts. What did they really know of dragons? Was trade a wise decision? And where would it lead?

* * *

The pearly light of a nearly full moon washed through the water. Scree pulsed toward the dragon shore, skimming the bottom in a close-knit formation with Orm, Spar, and the other octopus envoys. Together they resembled a larger, more formidable creature.

Spar had finally agreed to trade, so they would meet in late spring at the dragon shore. His eyes darted in all directions as he constantly scanned for danger, never even pausing to admire a rare fish. This continual alert made Scree nervous.

She glanced up at Tara, who swam far above with a large sack of seaweed and pearls attached to her shell. The huge sea turtle, grateful for Scree's healing, had become so helpful that she was almost indispensable.

A dark shadow slid across Scree.

She froze, perfecting her camouflage to match the sea floor. Her pod-mates also changed color. The large bull shark was hunting. It slowed and circled back. The pod should resemble a lumpy rock. But if they moved, it would see them.

The shark circled closer.

Scree could taste the metallic flavor of Orm's fear through the sea. She became a living rock, barely breathing, watching through slitted eyes. The shark swam even closer. Water pushed against her as it passed right above. She could count its sharp, jagged teeth.

Then, suddenly, the shark veered off and sped away in pursuit of something else. Scree shuddered. It was Tara, splashing noisily as she tried to flee. Of course she panicked. Tara lived with the scars of the last shark attack. She had a good lead, but the stream-lined shark was built for speed and it tore through the water.

The ungainly turtle was breathing hard, terrified, fins desperately churning. The gap between predator and prey was swiftly closing. This time, Tara would die.

NO!!

Scree dropped her healer's bag and jetted to intercept the shark. She smoothed her skin and molded her flexible head into a rounded point. She straightened and merged her arms together, streaming behind her, becoming a shark-shaped torpedo. Her muscular valve pulsed water like a jet. Scree moved incredibly fast for an octopus, carefully cutting the angle to reach Tara first.

Orm's eyes rounded with fear and his body shocked white. No octopus ever chased a shark! He quivered, hesitating. Then Orm dropped his sack and followed Scree, adapting his body for speed. He could not maintain this pace for long.

They converged on either side of the shark just as it reached Tara. Scree noticed Orm with surprise. He remembered the plan, and was helping despite his fears! Orm and Scree each managed to throw an arm onto the shark, suctioning to hold fast. Then they slung themselves forward through the water onto the shark's head and squirted ink into its eyes.

Distracted, the shark turned to confront its new prey.

Tara headed for an underwater ledge and disappeared into its shadow.

Scree and Orm flipped away from the shark's head, avoiding the jagged, pointed teeth. They fastened many arms onto the shark's back, the only safe place to hide, and held on. The predator flew through the water, swimming in circles, seeking its lost prey. Octopus arms were strained and bruised by the force of water pulling against them. Rough, sandpaper sharkskin shredded their softer skin.

As the shark neared Tara's hiding place, Orm and Scree released suckers and tumbled off its back, slipping under the ledge to join her. The shark circled once more and then headed away in search of new prey.

Tara flew to the surface, starved for air.

Scree and Orm pulsed in a ragged pattern back to their pod. They sank to the sand, battered and exhausted.

Orm's arms curled and uncurled convulsively. "What were you thinking!?!"

"I wasn't thinking. I only had time to react. But I had everything under control," she snapped back.

"Scree – that was a shark! We were barely hanging on!"

"Well, I couldn't let it attack Tara!"

Scree collapsed into a limp bundle. "We thought this through before. Sharks are powerful, but not terribly bright. Orm - you were brave to help."

"No, not brave. I was paralyzed by my old memories. Then I remembered your plan. It was absurd to even contemplate such a thing. I never thought you'd try it! But I couldn't let you face the shark alone."

Orm gradually grew calmer and twined his arms into Scree's. Then he quivered with laughter. "An octopus chasing a shark! Who would believe it? You were right, though. A sharp wit *is* more powerful than sharp teeth."

Scree relaxed against him, remembering their courtship. Orm had created a night sky of glowing tunicate stars on her ceiling. They feasted together under these stars on clams from his new shellfish farms.

Then Orm gave her a lovely piece of tentacle artwork. The driftwood was sanded into an abstract seascape with swells and hollows. Flavorful oils soaked the wood. Only an octopus, with tentacle arms full of multi-sensory suckers, could fully appreciate the artistry.

Scree had closed her eyes, running an arm along its surface, feeling the interwoven touch/taste sensations. There were overlapping layers with salty-sweet currents. A deeper hollow held the flavor of a rare seaweed.

Her eyes flew open. That was a matrimonial cave! What a clever proposal. Orm was traditional, but he was also creative. He even accepted her unusual, unappreciated wander-lust and love of stars. She had extended three arms, accepting his proposal. They were mated.

But they had become even more than mates. Orm had faced his greatest fear to help her.

Scree glanced up as Spar, their leader, approached. He

was trembling with anger. "Scree, that was risky. I'm glad for Tara's sake that it worked, but I am responsible for the entire pod. A long journey, away from the safety of our caves, is already dangerous enough. An octopus should not seek greater danger."

Scree barely controlled an instinctive flush of anger at his censure. She held herself rigid, unable to respond appropriately. How could he be so callous, so narrow-minded? Could he never see beyond his own tentacles? She could never have abandoned Tara to that shark, and her plan had worked.

Scree's rigid body seemed to show a respectful stance and Spar appeared to be mollified. He turned away and signaled an end to their break.

Scree twirled her arms in frustration. Spar excelled at organizing and protecting the pod. But there had to be more to life than avoiding danger. Helping a friend was certainly more important, and exploring beyond the narrow confines of their village. What was life without the beauty of crystal stars, and the satisfaction of healing in new ways?

* * *

Arak flew the storm, seeking likely bolts of lightning. He caught one with his copper claws and deftly threw it into the quartz sand on the dragon shore. Extreme heat melted the sand into a glass rod, a cast of the lightning's path. The crystal rods were harvested from the sand and polished with dragon fire. Lightning casts would be prime trade items.

Arak and Taron worked together at the steeper shore where clan and pod would gather. They put logs firmly into the bank at different depths. These sea seats would let octopi flow up or down with the changing tides.

Arak built one of the eight guest houses, below low tide near the flat beach. It had a circular base, stone walls, and a narrow entrance. He intertwined long pieces of branching coral, salvaged from storm debris, to make a sturdy roof. He filled mesh bags with shallow-water clams dug from the sand and placed these nutritious treats in the undersea homes.

Arak tried to think of every possible comfort. The trading festival had to run smoothly because, as the main interpreter, everything was riding on his wings. This was his chance to redeem himself after crashing on his solo. He flicked his tail nervously, hoping he wouldn't fail the clan or the pod.

Finally, it was the eve of the last full moon of spring. Fingers of the sea slapped the shore in a drum roll and slipped away with a sigh.

Arak stood in the restless surf, rustling his wings, full of nervous energy. Taron joined him and they stood together, peering out to sea, waiting.

"What have I forgotten?" Arak asked his friend anxiously, yet again.

Taron snapped his tail irritably. "Nothing! Everything will be fine! Now relax or you'll make us both crazy."

At sundown, a tangle of glistening arms surfaced near the beach. Eight golden dragons on the shore welcomed eight octopus envoys from the sea. Karana greeted Spar formally, while Arak and Scree twined arm and claw in friendship.

"How was the journey?" Arak asked.

"Rather mundane, except for the shark entertainment." Scree's eyes twinkled as she glanced at Orm.

He just smiled, refusing to rise to the bait.

Arak's eyes bulged. He was practically dying of curiosity, but a proper host would wait. "I'd like that story, but you must be exhausted. We'll talk tomorrow."

Arms dragging, clearly weary from their long journey, Orm and Scree slipped underwater to rest in a hospitable home with a generous meal.

* * *

The following dawn, Scree squirted to the surface, eager to see Arak's world for the first time. Warm air blew across her skin and unfamiliar tastes teased her sensitive suckers. A long white edge sparkled to the north. An ice floe? Why had it not melted like Arak's floe?

Towering brown and green reefs lay ahead in the distance. These must be the trees Arak had tried to describe. Their size was impressive, but they were not nearly as colorful or interesting as the pod's coral reefs. A few tiny, orange creatures swam among them. Were those butterflies?

Arak and Arafine greeted her enthusiastically.

Scree stared at the ice. "Is it always winter here?"

Arak shook his head. "That ice remains always, but in winter our whole world is covered with cold, white snow. This is spring, when trees grow new green leaves, a bit like kelp. Creatures mate and rainbow flowers appear." Arak gave Scree some pink and blue spring flowers. She felt the softness and tasted their delicate sweetness.

"It will soon be summer and the days will be hot. Fruits ripen and dragonlets hatch. Next comes autumn, when tree leaves turn ruby and gold like me." Arak stretched tall and his polished scales caught the early light. "Then the leaves fall off the trees."

"Do you have seasons?" Arafine asked, stretching and

re-folding her wings.

"The sea remains cool all year, but seasons do change below the waves," Scree replied. "We don't have trees that change colors, or a blanket of snow that hides the world. Changes in our world are hidden inside life. There are seasons to hatch, grow, mate, and release eggs, for all creatures."

That evening the clan and pod met to trade crystal and pearl treasures. Karana and Arafine rolled lustrous pearls in their claws while Kragor tried algae samples.

Scree ran eager arms along a crystal shaft. "These are perfect." She tasted one of the numerous packages of tea and her arms twisted with delight.

Trading was brisk. Scree and Arak helped translate at first, but soon the envoys could use the new language well enough to trade. Dragons and octopi worked together, making more sign-words as needed.

Scree sampled foods from land and sea in nightly feasts, while colorful dragon fires lit the shore. In response to questions about their home, the pod clustered together and imaged their coral reef. A rainbow fish swam realistically across Scree and then Orm, an embellishment perfected after much practice.

The dragons leaned forward and stared.

Scree smiled. Even Arak had never seen such an elaborate picture.

Scree helped Orm display oysters at different stages of growing pearls. Dragons crowded around as Orm demonstrated the culture procedure. He inserted a small shell ball into an oyster and covered it with a piece of living mantle cut from another oyster. The fleshy mantle normally grew the pearly inner surface of the shell, but now it would coat the ball with layers of pearl crystals.

Orm tried to explain the effect of diet on pearl color, but the dragons were obviously lost. So he held up a polished coral branch set with a circle of pearls: white, cream, orange, peach, pink, lilac, and black. "I can grow these colors."

Kragor thumped his tail. "That's the perfect mine. Rocks you can grow. We still need copper and all our searches have failed."

Orm nodded. "Crops are useful. We grow seaweed that is rich in iodine, to treat wounds. I'm still searching for seaweed that concentrates copper. We looked on our way here. Could we see dragon art?"

Kragor grinned. "I'd love to show you our ice sculptures, but that's only in winter. You'll like the amber ornaments."

Arafine and several dragon-ladies brought an impressive collection to the shore. "We grow snowflakes in the clouds and then place them on liquid pine sap," she explained. "The sap takes the flake patterns and we turn the sap into stone. It's faster than growing your pearls, but less shimmery."

Orm plucked up several ornaments. He peered through the warm, translucent stone. He felt the intricate, six-pointed patterns with his suckers and tasted the amber. One design was made of three eights of tiny dragons, another had fish, and two had creatures he couldn't identify.

"Amazing," Orm said. "Is real snow this beautiful?"

"Orm, you should join me on a northern journey to truly appreciate snow. It falls like rain, only softer and slower. But no natural snowflakes are as fanciful as these." Would Orm ever explore with her?

The following afternoon, Scree hovered safely below the waves with the pod, watching a storm-dark sky. Golden bodies flared brightly and disappeared as dragons tossed lightning in the storm clouds. Rainbow colors flashed in an electric display. Scree felt the rumbling thunder through the water. She slipped an arm above the wave and tasted the burnt air.

"This is stunning. Arak tried to explain the beauty of colored sky-fire, and decided it simply had to be seen. But even I think that storm-flying is too dangerous," Scree confided to Orm.

"So even you have limits?" He wriggled with laughter and reached an arm to his mate.

Scree batted it aside in irritation, but then twined arms as she remembered the shark. He had risked all to help her.

Language skills grew with each evening, and soon they could share simple stories. Arak raised his wings for attention. "Tell us about the shark."

Scree looked nervously at her leader. Spar glared angrily but signed his permission, unwilling to deny a direct request from their host. Arak stiffened and flicked his tail. Scree sighed. Spar was angry and Arak was worried about diplomacy. She decided to make the best of an inky situation.

Scree told the tale with skillful mimes, body pictures, and shape-shifting while dragons peered over the edge in rapt attention. They were clearly impressed that two small octopi would challenge a deadly shark. Scree finished with a flourish, resumed her normal shape and color, and flowed back onto her log seat.

Dragons thumped their tails enthusiastically and added various octopus signs of approval. Spar wore a peculiar expression, appearing both pleased by the clan's praise and irritated by any vindication of Scree's misdeed. Arak simply looked relieved.

All too soon, the festival was over. Tara arrived, ready to help again. Arak helped Scree load the huge turtle with bags of crystal lightning, tea and spices. He carefully checked the knots.

Scree nodded approvingly. "You managed this gathering very well."

"But I irritated your leader and our envoys didn't know the new language nearly as well as they should have," Arak replied, shaking his head. Sea foam clung to his scales, giving him a rather bedraggled appearance.

"Arak, nothing will ever be perfect." Scree pointed along the shore, where dragons and octopi still conversed. "Look. Nobody wants to leave. Karana and Spar are planning another trading festival for next spring. That is success, and you should be proud."

Arak brushed off the foam and managed an almost-happy smile.

Orm joined them, adding a sack of clams to the turtle's load. "Now we'll have enough journey food." He patted the turtle on her side, where the shell had been repaired, and looked at Scree.

"I hope our shark has found new hunting grounds!"

CHAPTER 5: WINTER FESTIVAL

Arak shivered with delight. A sea breeze blew across the field of musical ice sculptures, creating a symphony of sound. The Winter Festival was alive with music.

Abstract sculptures, the size of dragonlets, glistened like oddly-melted icebergs on a sea of blue-shadowed snow. The sculptures had hollow sections with small, carefully-spaced holes. These holes caught the wind, making chords and trills that blended together in dragonly melodies.

Arak smiled with satisfaction as he put the finishing touches on his own ice sculpture. After three days of painstaking work, it was finished. This was a realistic sculpture of Zarina's new medicinal herb. The thick, icy vine was a hollow spiral riddled with musical holes. Three flame flowers hung from the vine, each a cluster of ice petals, clinking like chimes.

Arak's sculpture was very different from the irregular ice shapes on the field. Would the clan like it? Maybe, next winter, there would be a whole meadow of whistling ice flowers!

Arak adjusted a few holes, widening some and closing others, tuning his vine to match the other sculptures. The sound blended perfectly. Light glinted off the textured stem and delicate flowers. Well, at least Zarina would like it. Arak left to find her.

Karoon strolled along the ocean edge of the festival and Arak automatically adjusted his course to avoid him. Nothing would mar this sparkling day. The mouth-watering aroma of roasting almonds drew Arak like flies to ripe fruit. He contentedly munched on a generous handful of warm, spiced nuts.

A high-pitched shriek split the air.

Arak spun toward the piercing sound. A first-year dragonlet plummeted down the long spiral ice slide, squealing with delight. The huge slide had been melt-carved into the glacier with dragon fire. The dragonlet opened her stubby wings as she neared the end of the slide, practicing near-flight on this impressive play-scape. She landed on a pile of soft snow, scrabbled off, and began toddling up the winding groove for another flying slide.

Arak closed his eyes. Cold wind tore by in his memories as he relived the ecstasy of his first plunge down a Winter Festival ice slide.

Arak looked up. Zarina vaned her wings as she hovered, holding almost motionless, high above in the peachy-gray snow clouds. They had tussled playfully as dragonlets, and now she was a dragon-lady growing her first cloud-sculpture.

Arak found a bench and waited for her to finish. Kragor joined him, waiting.

* * *

Four dragon-ladies clustered together companionably in the winter clouds. Zarina chose a tiny snowflake, growing inside its super-cooled sac of water. She delicately inserted the tip of a copper claw into the heart of the crystal cocoon. She would help it grow into a fantasy flake as big as a dinner plate.

Zarina pulsed electric energy into the center of the six-pointed crystal. Her snowflake caught new water molecules at each tip, keeping its symmetry. She briefly warmed the crystal sac to make the crystal tips grow thinner. She concentrated, carefully adding trace metals to manipulate the pattern. She controlled the crystal's growth to create a fanciful shape.

At last, the flake was finished. Zarina held a lacy network of tentacles with a head at each of the six points. Light sparkled along the crystals.

Driana glanced over with a look of surprise. She stopped pulsing energy into her own cloud sculpture. "An octopus snowflake! How original! The overlapping arms are perfect. Even as a dragonlet you had the necessary concentration. Growing snow crystals is a lot like growing crystals across a dragon's broken bone. You'll be a superb healer."

Arafine looked at Zarina's sea-flake. "It's unique. A frozen flake is a clever way to capture a water-being." She tilted her head, studying her own crystal kaleidoscope. The intricate design was entirely made of dragons.

Karana nodded approvingly. "Arafine, politics and personalities are woven together much like the dragons in your snowflake. I've been clan leader for four terms and it's time to fold my wings. I'd like to sponsor you as leader."

Arafine tilted her head, considering.

The dragon-ladies spiraled down from the clouds with their crystal creations. They landed near the Arak's bench.

Kragor stood up and peered at Arafine's dragon snowflake. "What exceptional detail."

Arafine beamed and twined necks with her mate.

Arak watched closely, then turned to compliment Zarina's octopus snowflake. "This is truly unique."

Zarina smiled. "I'd love to meet Scree. I'm glad she was there to help you."

Arak returned her smile, rustling his wings with a surge of energy, happily flicking the tip of his tail. He'd found the right thing to say! "I had a lucky accident. It was a thrill to meet such a different creature who thinks like a dragon. What an interesting mind! Scree loves to explore. She even loves stars and snow."

Arak stopped. He was babbling mindlessly.

Zarina hesitated. "Yes. Well, it's time to make the amber ornaments." She turned away, carrying her octopus snowflake on wide-spread claws.

Arak sighed in frustration. Why hadn't he invited Zarina to meet Scree? Her octopus design, her comment . . . it was the perfect opening. He decided to try again.

Arak followed Zarina to a large, smooth slab of limestone and watched over her shoulder. The rock had been coated with oil and spread with thin plates of melted pine sap. She put her icy creation onto a warm, liquid plate, and the cold snowflake made a perfect mould of itself as it hardened the sap. A crackling zap of electricity turned the golden sap into amber. She carefully trimmed her gem-flake with a sharp claw and held it up to the light.

Arak cleared his throat nervously. "Zarina, your ornament has a beautiful pattern."

"Thanks. The symmetry is natural, but it was a challenge to grow curved arms."

A huge old hemlock tree soared above them, festooned with exquisite amber ornaments to celebrate the winter solstice. Zarina snapped her wings, flew up, and hung her intricate artwork on a suitable branch. She landed back beside him.

"Have you seen the musical sculptures?" Arak asked.

Zarina shook her head. "Not yet, but I promised to collect more wild snowflakes for the air ball games. The dragonlets keep breaking their flake-balls."

"Could you come just for a moment? Please?"

Arak eagerly led her to the field. They walked together amongst the oddly-shaped sculptures, bathed in humming notes that blended together like a chorus of tireless dragons. Arak listened closely to Zarina, trying hard to produce appropriate, perhaps even witty, responses. Lost in conversation, they quickly reached the edge.

Arak reared back, shocked. His perfect sculpture was a pile of glassy shards.

Karoon stood nearby, expertly juggling three ice balls.

"What do you know of this?" Arak demanded sharply. He eyed the flying balls, absolutely certain that Karoon had destroyed his sculpture.

Karoon smoothly added a fourth ball to his routine. He inclined his head toward Zarina with a warm smile and an elegant bow, never losing the juggling pattern. "Always a pleasure to see you, Za-ri-na." Her name rolled off his tongue like sweetened tea.

Karoon turned lazily to Arak and glanced down at the

shattered ice. "It looked kind of fragile, and it didn't really fit in, did it?" he answered noncommittally. "Like you," he mouthed to Arak as Zarina turned to poke among the ruins.

"This flower chime's nice," she said, giving it a gentle shake. It seemed to be the only unbroken part.

"But I sculpted that healer's herb you talked about. It was a complete flame-flower vine, with three flower chimes, and the notes were perfect, and . . ." Arak stopped, furious and hurt, struggling to control his emotions. He had to remain calm and mature in front of Zarina. And he would *not* give Karoon any more satisfaction. ". . . I thought you'd like it."

"I'm sorry, Arak. I'm sure it was lovely. But the dragon-ladies are expecting my help, and I really do have to go now." Zarina launched into the sky.

Karoon's eyes followed Zarina until she disappeared among the clouds. Then, using his foot, he prodded the ruins of Arak's sculpture. He grinned maliciously.

Arak flexed his claws, desperately wanting to fight, but there were stiff penalties for disturbing a festival. His nemesis was older and larger. Arak would lose and then be punished severely for striking the first blow. Even worse, his dam was responsible for discipline. It was so unfair!

He leapt into the sky and flew high, alone with his hurt, letting his fiery anger bleed into the frigid gray clouds. Three days! He'd worked on his sculpture for three days, and Zarina didn't even get to see it! Only the broken shards and his near-meltdown. He buried himself deeper in thick, swirling shadows.

Arak was half frozen when he landed. He vented the remnants of his rage by raking his claws through the crusty snow. Sparkling ice crystals flew up, reminding him of a wild slide-ride with Taron last winter. They had careened down a steep, icy slope onto the frozen stream, spinning dizzily, totally out of control.

Taron was always ready to have fun! This could still be a terrific day. When he found his friend, Arak's eyes bulged in disbelief.

"What are you doing?"

"Managing the air-ball games," Taron replied, as if he was always so mature and helpful. The lacy "flake-balls" had snowflake sides that fitted together. Zarina had probably made one of them, using large wild flakes harvested in the clouds.

"That's it! You're doing great!" Taron cried. "Keep that ball in the air! Careful, don't let it break!" Second-year dragonlets ran a course while keeping a fragile ball in the sky, blowing puffs of air and using carefully-aimed wing buffets. This was more exercise than game. It developed lung strength and wing agility, both essential for flying.

The dragonlets were clearly disinterested, making only half-hearted attempts to keep the ball up. Arak had to agree with them: nothing could be more boring than air-ball.

"We're going to the ice slide next," Taron said. "You could help."

They'd love the impressive ice slide. Arak could help, but he didn't really want to watch the youngsters enjoying that incredible ride. Not when he secretly wished to join them.

"Will you be done after the slide?" Arak asked hopefully.

Taron shook his head. "Erinite recruited me, and I promised to help until dinnertime."

Arak flicked his tail in frustration. After dinner it

would be too late for anything fun.

Erinite arrived with her tired group from the ice slide. She greeted Arak cheerfully before affectionately rubbing heads with Taron. "Your turn." She whispered something in Taron's ear. He laughed and herded his eager charges to the slide.

Arak mumbled a hasty farewell and stumbled away, hardly looking where he was going. Why was it so easy for Taron and Erinite to be together? And why was it so hard for him to do anything with Zarina?

Arak looked up and stared. A dragon-lord was being marched off to the cave. Banned from the feast! What had he done? Arak recognized the glint of copper in a large bowl, carried by the clan official. Hoarding. Copper was for everyone, but dragons got nervous when there was a shortage. Arak felt rather sorry for the culprit.

Bright flames lit the edge of the festival. Young dragons practiced flaming small branches sunk in the snow. An old dragon-lord, bronzed with age, explained, "Body scales are tough, but wings can be hurt by flames. That's why we practice on snow or on the beach. If you misjudge the wind, fire can be quickly extinguished and . . ."

"And this prevents accidental ground fires," Arak finished quietly, remembering his early lessons.

As a youngster he had delighted in breathing a torrent of fire, the bigger the better. But now he was older and had precision control. He blew a circle of flame, melting a perfect ring in a smooth patch of snow. Then he pursed his mouth and added thin wavy melt-lines to the circle, drawing an intricate octopus with fire.

Arak tilted his head, studied the design, and smiled. He added five more octopi to complete Zarina's snowflake.

Arak straightened his wings. Zarina was clearly interested in octopi, and there was something that only he could do. He would definitely invite Zarina along for his next visit to Scree. Smiling cheerfully, Arak headed for the inner-vision ice sculptures.

Arak reached the ring of huge ice blocks cut from the glacier. A crowd of dragons watched Kragor breathe rivers of flame onto a translucent opal-blue block, melting it into a beautiful, abstract shape.

Arak's smile faded. What would it be like, to be surrounded by admirers? Not that musical sculptures were ever valued as highly as inner-vision ice. But he'd worked hard on his sculpture, creating something completely new, and no one had even seen it!

Kragor added curved facets to the ice and stepped away, giving his sculpture a critical glance. These facets focused sunlight to create luminous internal images, like a complex star sapphire. When the sun reached the right angle in the sky, light came through a constellation of facets and a light sculpture appeared in the ice.

Kragor's four-dimensional artwork changed across time. Many overlapping scenes lay dormant, invisible in the solid ice. Only one image could be clearly seen at any given time. The moving sun gradually revealed each new glowing design hidden within the ice.

Kragor's work was clearly the best. It was as if he captured the aurora borealis and molded it into a vision.

"There you are!" Kragor said happily to Arak. "It's finished. Come watch the ice images with us."

Arak came inside the ring of sculptures and sat on one of the welcoming seats woven from springy branches. As the sun slowly crossed the sky, images appeared and faded in each of the fancifully carved blocks of ice. There were scenes from travels, legends and lives. Watching ice images with his parents was a poor second to the excitement of sliding down the ice path with friends. But Zarina was helping Erinite and Taron was grilling fish.

Arak saw himself emerge from the egg in Kragor's ice sculpture. Next he flew down an ice slide. In the afternoon sunlight, a larger Arak made his first flight.

A cluster of dragons oohed and aahed over the exquisite detail. Arak rustled his wings irritably, jealous of Kragor's admirers. It didn't help that all of the ice-images were lovingly focused on Arak; he now felt small and petty as well.

"These are like watching a dream," Arafine sighed as an even larger Arak filled the ice, leaving on his first solo flight.

Arak quietly closed his eyes, shutting out the image. That flight was not exactly a dream journey! Karoon found subtle ways to remind everyone that Arak had crashed. Yes, he had met a strange alien. But he had not found copper, which was what *really* mattered.

Everyone worried about copper. The mine was almost empty, there was still no new source, and copper was rationed. A few selfish dragons hoarded copper, which was forbidden, while others shared their copper rations with the sick and needy. When dragons suffered from copper deficiency their golden scales turned orange. Their joints became stiff and painful, making it hard to fly. The copper problem was impossible to ignore but, during a festival, dragons focused on fun.

"The feast is almost ready," Arafine said.

Arak inhaled deeply, savoring the scents. He could

hardly wait. Enticing aromas of traditional spiced fish and roasted tubers permeated the air, layered with more exotic smells. He played a game of sorting the scents, identifying each individual food.

The sun sank lower, painting the sky with amethyst and indigo. The sun would not set all the way, so their festival would be beautifully dark-lit all night long. Sparkling ice frosted the thick winter blanket that covered the land. The ice reflected the sky, surrounding the clan in a liquid display of color.

The brass dinner gong rang loudly across the silent snow. Arak flew to the long stone tables, racing the other eager dragons.

The traditional main course was a thick, spicy fish stew. There were side dishes of steaming rock crab claws, stuffed clams, thick roasted tubers, sweet dried berries, salted pine nuts, and ornate platters with whorls of pale slivered nuts on fresh brown seaweed. Roasted almonds and steamed oysters were each a minor food source of copper.

The platters of sweet mashed yams were edible masterpieces, decorated with ground gemstones. Vibrant designs were made from green malachite and turquoise; each gem had some copper. The patterns were like a burst of green and blue lightning.

Arak filled his plate, sampling all the delights.

After he ate, Arak scrubbed his plate with snow and stacked it on the shelf under the table. Then he chose a traditional dessert: snow pudding, a luscious treat made only for their Winter Festival. Blue-green snow, laden with algae, had a delicate floral flavor. This rare seasonal snow was mixed with fresh Sturgeon eggs.

Arak took a bite and his eyes lit with pleasure. The snow pudding was even more tasty than usual, laid on a bed of succulent red seaweed. Red seaweed! That rare, tasty garnish came from trade with octopi, and he had made that happen. He savored the dessert and lifted his head higher.

Arak fiddled with his empty bowl.

Tomorrow he would work with Taron and Zarina on the trance-mind exercises. He'd really looked forward to this chance to be with Zarina. But when she made the octopus snowflake he'd rambled on nervously about Scree. He totally missed her obvious interest in an invitation, and she'd given him an odd look. And then the sculpture fiasco.

What must she think of him?

CHAPTER 6: DRAGON FLAMES

"My eyes are burning," Arafine said to Driana. It was the morning after the feast.

Driana checked her eyes. "Any other problems?" Arafine had no appetite, unheard of for a dragon. This was neither indigestion nor injury, the most common complaints.

Driana finished her tests. "Your scent is normal, indicating no nutrient deficiencies. Wing color is good, so metal balance should be fine. Eyes are too bright, but there's no fever or nausea to indicate flu. This matches nothing I've ever seen, or heard of."

Four more dragons came in with the same symptoms.

Driana investigated the possibility of food poisoning, but they'd eaten different dishes at the festival. Every dragon had eaten the traditional snow pudding, but only a few were ill. Later that day her patients were shaking, miserable, and unable to feed. Their eyes grew even brighter. The dragons were beginning to waste away, and Driana was no closer to a diagnosis.

* * *

Arak, Taron and Zarina flew to an isolated spot to practice the trance-mind. He chose a quiet place near a limestone cliff, protected from the wind. The sheer stone wall was completely covered with tangled icicles, gleaming like a thousand crystal suns.

"Another day, another trance," Taron said.

"It's a useful skill," Arak said. He had mastered mind-to-mind communication long ago, but his friends needed practice.

Dragons began with simple trance-mind exercises; distance and detail improved over the years, with practice. This skill allowed the clan to stay in contact wherever they traveled. A clan official entered the trance-mind each sunrise and sunset, ready to communicate with distant dragons.

Arak watched Zarina secretly. They'd been friends forever, but everything was changing. She was now a dragon-lady, and could choose a mate. Most healers remained single to better concentrate on their work, but Zarina seemed interested in dragonlets. If she chose a mate, who would it be? Karoon was showing a real interest in her. He was one season older than Arak and could appear quite charming.

Arak shivered. He just could not stand it if she chose Karoon!

His tail drooped. He should partner with Zarina for these exercises, but he could barely talk to her sensibly with dragon-words. He might make a real fool of himself in trance. Arak shuddered at the thought. He chose Taron.

Zarina stood guard. "I hear the scrabbling of dweer, but it's far off. There's no immediate threat."

Arak and Taron took out their trance stones and prepared to meditate.

Arak sank deeper into trance as he stilled his mind and focused into his translucent aquamarine globe. He felt peaceful, calm nothingness as he looked down on his body. His trance-mind spied the shimmer that should be Taron's. As the shimmers overlapped, he heard Taron's voice as if from a cave, deep within his mind. The inner voice was a flat monotone.

Arak, would you like to ice fish

Yes. Would you like to partner with Zarina next

Why. She likes you, not me

Arak nearly lost control of his trance. Was Taron teasing him? Then, unexpectedly, they were joined by a third trance-mind.

This is Karana. Come to the clinic

Their leader's thought-message was shared with calm urgency.

Arak returned to his body, worried. It was against tradition to interrupt the trance-mind exercises, because it was so important to develop this skill. "I wonder what the problem is. If there's a clinic emergency, why not just ask for Zarina, the healer-in-training?"

"Has everyone been called?" Taron wondered aloud. "Who was hurt?"

The trio flew to the dragon clinic, racing the wind. They landed near five sickly dragons, each sprawled limp on a pallet.

Arak shuddered in disbelief. NO!!! Arafine lay among

them. He had never seen his dam so listless, and she didn't even greet him. This wasn't like her at all!

Zarina immediately set to work helping Driana, bathing the patients' eyes and tucking extra blankets around them. Driana explained that they weren't eating and didn't have enough energy to keep warm. She had no idea what was wrong, and they were rapidly getting worse.

Arak felt a growing desperation. This couldn't be happening! Driana was their healer, and she always knew what to do! He laid his head next to Arafine and whispered, "You can't just die. I still need you."

Kragor welcomed Arak, touching foreheads.

Arak blinked, startled. His sire had neither groomed his wings nor polished his scales. But Kragor *always* took pride in his appearance. Arak was lost in a white fog of fear. There was a high buzzing sound in his head. He heard a voice, as if from a great distance.

"I'm doing everything I can but it isn't enough," Driana said. "Scree has different healing and testing skills. Perhaps she could help."

Arak's mind cleared at the mention of Scree and a fragile hope blossomed. "I can fly her here," he said.

But it was a long flight there and back. Would Scree risk traveling out of water? And could he manage, with the extra burden of an octopus?

* * *

Scree felt the distinctive crash of the summoning stone. Only a dragon could lift it from the raft and drop it into the sea, to strike the rock below. It was not the full moon, not a standard time for dragon visits. There must be a problem. She grabbed her bag and headed for the raft, followed closely by her apprentice, Stur. Orm joined them.

They surfaced by the raft and climbed onto log seats, looking up at Arak and Taron.

Scree stared. She had never seen Arak so agitated. His wings furled and unfurled, his tail flicked and his claws clicked. It was as if all the restless tides of the sea were gathered together in him.

"Scree, five dragons are seriously ill. Arafine is dying and Driana can't identify the problem. We need you!"

"I have my healer's bag," Scree replied. "Orm, would you come, too? You're a terrific investigator, and I could use your help."

Arak bowed deeply, gratitude and relief shining in his eyes. "Time is crucial. Would you ride on my back? I've been experimenting with a safe way for you to fly. I made special capes to keep you wet and protect against the wind. I have two. I hoped you might both come."

Scree gazed up at the sunset and emerging stars. "We could fly with the stars! It would be like riding the shark, but more interesting."

Orm smiled with wry humor. "I'm not sure I can handle much more excitement than that shark. But if you're willing to try, so will I."

Arak thumped his tail. He unrolled the hooded capes and dipped them into the sea. The inner lining was woven from a soft, spongy plant that held water. The outer layer was cut from leathery fish skin.

Scree said to Stur, "You will be pod healer while I'm gone." They twined arms in friendship.

Scree fastened the wet cape below her head, flipped the hood over her head, and climbed onto Arak's back. The hood, with its two large eyeholes, settled over her face.

Orm pulled himself up onto Taron's back and settled

between the wings.

Both dragons leapt into the sky, wings beating hard. Scree fastened every suction cup firmly onto dragon scales. She flew faster than a spinning octopus in the wheel dance, surging up and down like the waves with each wing beat. The wind whipped past, pushing the cape against her body.

Scree looked down at the sparkling sea, but from such heights it looked endless, flat and barren. No one would guess that there was a whole world hidden below the waves. The coral reefs around her home had more color and life than a dragon forest. Everything was vibrant and beautiful, through all the seasons.

Moonbeams slid across her cape. She leaned back and flipped off her hood, gazing up at the night sky. High above the misty sea, stars shone with unexpected brilliance. Scree felt that she could reach out and pluck glittering gems from the night sky.

But the sky disappeared when she sank below the waves, and only the light reached into the sea. There were no crystal stars, no flaming sunsets. Their worlds were so different that it was truly surprising how well dragons and octopi got along.

The stars began to fade in the sky. Arak was trembling and breathing hard. His wing strokes were less even. Where was the shore? Just when Scree thought Arak might crash, they made a rough landing at the clinic shore.

Scree slipped off his back.

Arak greeted his dam and received a vacant stare. Arafine's feverish eyes were as bright as dragon flames, but it was obvious that she saw nothing of this world. Arak's sire lay in an untidy heap nearby.

Arak turned to Scree. Their eyes met and she bowed in

sympathy, adding the sign for hope.

Scree consulted with the head healer, Driana. Then she placed one arm on Arafine's wrist and one on Driana's, for a direct comparison of sick and healthy adult dragon-ladies. Her sensitive suckers tested for subtle differences in temperature, pulse, scent, texture, taste.

Scree closed her eyes, feeling every slight difference, seeking one that mattered. She turned to Orm. "There's a difference in trace metals, but I can't pinpoint the problem. This is your specialty. You used trace metals in those oyster diet experiments. Could you try?"

Orm flowed into place and used his octopus arms to repeat Scree's comparison. He appeared frozen in complete concentration. Then his eyes widened in surprise. "I've identified the problem! One batch of metal supplements killed my oysters. It was contaminated with thallium, a rare toxin. Arafine has thallium poisoning."

Scree's tense arms became limp seaweed. "This poison is very dangerous, but I know how to treat it. I need big containers of the blue-green snow that has algae."

Kragor gathered enough snow to make an iceberg. He melted it with rivers of dragon-fire, filling a huge cauldron. He could not do enough to help.

Scree made a broth for the sick dragons. She concentrated the snow-algae and adding thick, gelatinous seaweed to the mix. She explained as she worked: "The algae will bind with the thallium and help remove it. This seaweed will ease muscle pains."

She filled a bowl and motioned to Arak, who was restlessly rocking from foot to foot. "Arak, could you heat this bowl until it steams? We take our medicine cold, but dragons need the warmth."

Arak and Kragor took turns eagerly spooning the steaming broth into Arafine.

A bright green aurora borealis shimmered in the night sky, lighting the clinic. Driana brought snacks and steaming mugs of tea for all the helpers. Arak took a sip, then a longer drink. "This is really good! What do you do that's different?"

"It's the herbs. And the copper tea pot." Driana sighed. "This pot is a reserve supply for the clan. If we don't find copper soon, I'll have to grind it for supplements."

Arak nodded. "We'll search again soon. This time we plan to reach the far beaches."

Orm tested the food and metal seasonings. One shaker of sea salt was mixed with ground turquoise from a new mine. It was tainted with thallium. Kragor gave a deep sigh. "Turquoise is a poor substitute for pure copper, but we're desperate. We need every bit of copper we can find."

Orm made a fire test, since dragons could not sense the poison. When powdered turquoise was burned, the flames showed a purple tinge if it had thallium.

Four days later, Arafine regained her appetite and lost the feverish sheen in her eyes. Her muscles still ached. "Keep drinking the broth for another moon. The symptoms should fade away," Scree reassured.

Arak's eyes gleamed. He was practically dancing with joy. He stretched and folded his wings energetically as he talked with his dam, who now clearly saw and heard. Kragor's scales were again brightly polished and he held his head high, bringing yet another tasty food dish to tempt his mate. Arafine's hollow cheeks had begun to fill out again.

Scree relaxed at the water's edge, watching. She

flushed a cheerful green color, pleased that Arafine's recovery had healed three dragons.

Driana stepped forward, bowing formally to both Orm and Scree. "We're in your debt. What can we do for you?"

Orm gazed longingly at the distant white edge of the glacier, near the carved blocks of ice. "Could I see the ice sculptures?"

Kragor threw his head back and roared with laughter. The deep booming sound rocketed across the ice; Scree felt it ring through her body.

Kragor reached down to Orm, for the double clasp of friendship. "You are a kindred spirit, and I'll gladly take you. I'd love to see your glowing mosaics someday."

Arak approached, wings crisply folded, and gave Scree a small fishing spear. "I made this for you. Your healer skills are superb, but your teeth are unimpressive. This sharp tooth might be useful."

* * *

Scree slipped off Arak's back and looked around. Moonlit waves lapped against the logs of the new raft, which was anchored half-way between her octopus village and the dragon shore. Scree and Orm had dragon-flown to the raft to light a trial signal fire.

Arafine and other dragons would have died without Scree and Orm. The poisoned mine would have killed even more. Kragor and Arak were deeply grateful, and they designed this special raft so octopi could contact dragons.

A ceramic bowl full of plant wax, with a stick of fatwood in the middle, was lashed to the top of a tall pole. This bowl would hold the fire. Tanned fish skin was spread below to protect the wood raft from sparks.

Orm gazed up at the bowl, arms curling with concern.

"Fire that burns. I've lived in the sea all my life, and I'm not sure I'll ever get used to it. Dragon fires are beautiful, but I prefer the cold fire of my tunicates."

Scree followed his gaze and twined a comforting arm with Orm. "I love the tunicate sky you made on my ceiling, glowing like stars in the night. But, a fire we can start. That's amazing! If we ever need the dragons, this could be useful."

Scree and Orm together pulled a long, tough rope woven from fish skin. This rubbed flint against a star-stone, making a spark that lit the fatwood wick. Dragon flames twisted and grew.

Scree observed carefully as Arak slipped into trance-mind to contact Zarina on the shore. That would be a useful skill.

Arak seemed to awaken into his body. "They can see it! Now, dragons will stand watch at night for an octopus signal fire."

Orm bowed formally. "Thank you." He pulled another cord that dumped a bucket of sea water over the flame. The bucket was refilled and raised on a pulley.

Scree was silent, lost in thought. She studied the raft and pole, felt the wind against her skin, then eyed Arak's wings and the fish-skin. Everything clicked into place.

"Arak, I have an idea. We could make a tiny raft with a pole, and a fish-skin wing that can be moved. Then an octopus could fly on the water with the wind."

Arak's golden tail flicked up and down, as it often did when he was deep in thought. He looked down at Scree and snapped his wings excitedly. "It's a novel concept, but this could work! A triangle wing might be best."

Stars shifted overhead as time flew by, and at last they

had a workable skiff design. Scree flashed a picture of a shark across her body, with open jaws and impressive triangle teeth. "If this works, octopi will have a safer way to travel."

* * *

Scree waited impatiently with Orm at the edge of the first raft. She was coiled like a spring, watching eagerly as two golden specks grew larger in the sky. She could hardly stand the suspense. Arak and Taron flew unevenly toward them, straining against tow ropes. A skiff, about the size of a dragon, bounced on the waves behind them.

Arak landed on the raft. "What do you think?"

"I can't wait to try water-flying." Scree slid off her seat and climbed aboard. The skiff had a distinctive taste/feel of oak trees, unlike the pine log raft.

Scree moved the skiff-wing to catch the wind, but the skiff just slipped all over the place. She struggled to turn it with no success, and was blown further from the raft. Frustrated and dejected, she dropped the skiff-wing.

Arak flew to the skiff, seized a rope, and pulled her back to the raft.

"I can't control it," Scree sighed.

Orm took a closer look at the skiff. "Scree, remember the shark? The skiff needs a fin on the bottom to catch the water. And it should be more pointed in front, like a shark's nose. A skiff needs to be half shark, half dragon to properly fly on the water."

Arak and Taron brought a new skiff during the next full moon, and Zarina came along to visit. Scree and Orm took turns with the skiff. It worked much better, but they still had trouble making it go where they wanted.

Zarina peered at the skiff. "It needs another fin on the

back end like a fish tail, and a handle to move the tail."

Arak thumped his tail approvingly. "That's what it needs!"

Orm studied it again. "If the skiff has sides, it can hold water and keep us properly wet."

"Third time's the charm, I hope," Taron said.

Taron was right. The third skiff flew like a dream.

Scree, Orm and Stur took turns practicing beneath a silver moon. Dark rose and violet blossomed on the horizon, fading to pale blue as the sky lightened. Winged dragon shadows appeared on the raft as the sun climbed higher.

At last, Scree moored the skiff to the raft. Tired but triumphant, octopi and dragons clasped tentacle to claw and returned to their homes.

Arak and Taron found a new passion experimenting with skiff designs.

Scree and Stur studied the medicinal use of poison.

Orm covered another room with glowing tunicate designs.

Then, as the sun rose, their world changed forever.

CHAPTER 7: THE SEA BOILS

Arak awoke to the blackness of night before dawn and looked around uneasily. He slid off his comfortable pallet, dragging some leaves with him. He sniffed the air, finding no strange odors. He heard no dragons moving. In fact, he heard nothing at all. It was nearly springtime. Where were the crickets?

He crawled out of his small shelter, tucked beneath thick bushes at the base of a tree. It seemed a night like any other. But there were no crickets, and the air felt stiff.

Arak closed his eyes and turned slowly in a circle, reaching out with magnetic sight. Far out to sea, beyond the dimly lit horizon, gold sparks shot into the sky. What could that mean? Fear ran up his spine like an icy claw. He had to know. Arak focused through his gem and dove into trance. There was not even time to protect the helpless limp body he left behind.

His trance-mind flew far overseas, south of Scree's

village. A huge turtle was frantically swimming away. Below the place of sparks was a circle of roiling water, bubbling like a tea kettle. An undersea volcano!

Arak fled back into his body. He opened his eyes and shook off the trance, running to the gathering circle before he was fully awake. He pounded the huge signal drum.

Danger! Danger! Danger!

If only his signal could reach Scree! Her village was deep. Would that save the pod? There was no time to fly there. He could only warn the clan. In distant legends, when a sea mountain exploded the sea rushed inland. It would destroy the dragons.

Dragons crawled out of their various shelters and stumbled bleary-eyed to the circle.

Arak stilled the drum with a trembling hand. He stared out to sea. He could almost see the eruption, and the fearsome wall of water that would follow.

The clan muttered angrily as they woke fully.

"What's wrong? Bad dream? That's no reason to wake us," growled a dragon, raking his sharp claws through the sand with a menacing glare.

"Go back to sleep. It's just Dreamer," hissed another.

Arak filled his lungs and shouted, "There is danger! The volcano will erupt and the sea will come in!"

"What volcano?" Their mountain was quiet, with none of the smoke or smells described in legends.

Arak pointed. "Under the sea! Close your eyes and look. The sky sparkles like a storm with no clouds!" He spoke urgently, desperate to convince them.

"That is odd. But how can you know what it means?" asked an elder, in a calm, reasonable voice.

As if he was an addled dragonlet. Arak snapped his tail

angrily, but he was afraid to tell. After years of teasing, he never spoke of the trance-mind. The clan didn't know his secret. Only he could see more than just his body or another trance-mind. Only he could truly see the danger. They called him Dreamer. How could he prove that it wasn't a dream?

"I just know," Arak said stubbornly. "We must leave now."

Karana, their leader, pulled him aside and asked quietly, "How do you know?"

He squirmed uneasily before replying, in a low voice, "Below the sparks, the sea boils. The volcano lives. We just can't see it from here."

Karana studied him in silence. "You saw this? How?" She searched his face. "In trance-mind?" She sounded incredulous.

He fumbled with his claws and nodded. "I see more than minds. It's a bit blurry, but I see what's really there. That's why I quest. I can't prove this and I don't want to explain it to them. I'm already called the trance-freak."

He saw belief in her eyes. Karana nodded solemnly and turned to the crowd.

"We must leave. Go to the top of the far hill, beyond the stream. The sea should not reach us there." Karana assigned dragons to move the dragonlets. "The rest of you, take what we'll need most: copper, food, water, clinic supplies. If there's time we'll make extra trips. Now load up and fly!"

Arak flew to the clinic to move crucial healer supplies, hoping they wouldn't need these. Zarina was wrestling with a heavy load. "Here, I'll take that." Fear lent him the strength of many dragons. He added a big stack of blankets and tied the entire load to his back, between his wings. He soared off to the hills, unloaded, and returned.

It was early dawn when Arak fastened his second load. He looked out to sea, noting the clear sky and calm, normal waves. He closed his eyes, checking again with inner sight. A powerful burst of magnetic sparks shot high into the sky. The hidden volcano had erupted! How much time did they have before the sea charged in?

*   *   *

The sea floor rumbled and shuddered, rousing Scree from her dreams. She automatically grabbed her healer's bag and crawled shakily from her cave, waking quickly as she surveyed the damage. A cloud of small silver fish swam erratically, unable to maintain their normal precision schooling.

Her world shook again.

Shock-waves rushed through the water, knocking Scree head-over-tentacles. Octopi spilled out of their trembling caves, seeking the safety of the open dance floor. They were bruised and disoriented, convulsively curling their arms.

Scree avoided a swarm of agitated, stinging jellyfish as her eyes searched the gathering crowd. It was hard to see through the roiled, cloudy water. Orm squirted forward and grasped her arms; she could feel his intense relief through their embrace.

Orm looked down at her bag. "You're amazing! You never forget that, no matter what."

A huge manta ray swam by with slow, uneven strokes, favoring a torn wing fin.

"I'm afraid I'll truly need it this time," she replied gravely.

The undersea volcano cast an eerie glow in the far distance. Red lava sparked up through the sea, turning to black grit as it showered down.

Spar, the leader, flowed to the top of the nearest cave to survey the damage. A huge head of coral had shattered and, more ominously, several caves had collapsed. He addressed his pod, "Is anyone missing?"

* * *

Arak checked the sea again, as he fastened his third load. He stared. The sea was draining away from the shore! Crabs pranced frantically on the exposed rocks, and he could see the octopus guest-homes. Long strands of seaweed lay flat, pointing toward the disappearing water like accusing fingers.

Arak yelled, "Fly! Now!"

Moments later the sea rushed back to the shore. Water piled together, growing into a fearsome wall many dragon-lengths tall. The noise was beyond belief.

Arak flew above the towering wall that raced inland, past the shoreline. It crested into a hungry wave and passed below him, faster than any dragon. Heading for their hill. He watched the water tear trees from the ground as easily as he could toss a twig. Nothing could stand against it! The huge wave slapped against their hill with more force than an iceberg hitting the sea.

Arak held his breath as the roiling water surged higher and higher, reaching for the exhausted clan. Would it ever stop?

Finally the wave hesitated. It slid back, clawing the sides of the hill as it left, raking bushes and boulders from the ground. The powerful, greedy undertow grabbed everything in its path, dragging it into the sea. The snarling water subsided. Arak reached the hilltop and collapsed onto the ground. He wearily loosened the straps on his back and let his heavy load slide to the ground. It was over.

Arak stared in dismay. A new wave rose up and roared inland, scouring the land. But it did not reach the height of the first devastating wave. A third wave slashed at the base of the hill. The sea sloshed across the land several more times before retreating to its proper place.

Arak took a deep breath, smelling salty soil and pungent, torn leaves. The land was covered with mud and debris. Seaweed and driftwood clung to the tops of the few surviving trees. Toppled giants bobbed in the surf. The clinic tents were gone. Everything they left behind was gone.

Karana sat down beside him, looking as weary as he felt, and bowed her head respectfully. "Everyone is safe. We even had time to save what's left of our copper. Without your warning . . ." She looked meaningfully at the scoured hillside and floating trees. "Your extraordinary trance abilities are a gift to be proud of. But I won't tell."

* * *

Scree shivered with fear. Three octopi were missing. She and her apprentice, Stur, went with neighbors to check their homes.

Krel was seriously wounded right beneath his head. Scree immediately bandaged the wound and gave him an herb to slow the bleeding. Meanwhile, four octopi worked together to free a young female who was pinned by a large stone. Two arms were crushed, and these would have to be amputated.

"Take them to my cave," Screc ordered. "Stur, prepare the patients."

Scree trembled when they reached the last cave. It had been reduced to a pile of rubble and Tron, her life-long friend, lay beneath the rocks. She grabbed a stone and heaved it aside. Others joined her, grabbing and tossing. They worked with desperate efficiency, daring to hope that Tron lay in a protected pocket. When the last rocks were removed, Scree shuddered and flushed gray. His body was crushed.

Tron was dead.

Scree held perfectly. Unable to accept the loss, her mind wandered through living memories. She saw Tron bringing her turquoise rocks for healing. He spoke excitedly of a world with huge white crabs and clear fish, discovered on a northern trip. Tron waved a cheerful greeting at the New Moon Festival.

An arm gently touched Scree, bringing her back to the present like a jolt from an electric eel. She saw Tron's body and painful reality flooded in. Never again would she watch his perfect mimicry of the king crab dance. Never again would they discuss the inexplicable lure of faraway places. Tron had been a rare kindred spirit.

Scree bowed sadly to her old friend. She turned away and headed for her cave. The wounded were waiting.

The patients lay in her outer chamber. Her apprentice would have a rare opportunity to practice some special healer skills. "Stur, give Krel a mild sedative. We can't risk more. I'd like your help repairing this tear."

Scree used a strong anesthetic on the youngster, who soon dropped into a deep sleep. "It will be awkward for her to move on only six, but the two arms that I must amputate should regrow within a year." Scree sharpened her black garnet knife on a whetstone.

After the operations, Stur crushed fragrant seaweed to fill the small room with a pleasant, relaxing taste.

Spar was busy, efficiently organizing crews to repair damaged homes and clean up debris. Scree found him and, as pod healer, gave her report.

A large dead fish drifted down beside them.

"It's ironic. I worried about our journey to the dragon shore, but the true danger was here, at home," Spar said. "I suppose everything has its risks and benefits."

An active volcano was a distant legend, almost beyond memory. There had been no eruption in countless generations, but undersea volcanic vents continually warmed the water. This allowed their coral reef to grow further north in nutrient-rich waters, at latitudes that would normally be too cold.

There were no more after-shocks, so they uneasily returned to their caves. Later, the pod held a ceremony for the dead. Scree and Orm joined the line of friends behind Tron's body. Each friend imaged a special memory of him. Then they covered his body with branches of dead coral. The entire pod planted seaweed around the coral, until colorful strands covered the small new reef. Soon the sea would reclaim him.

Tron's name was etched in a round, dark gray volcanic rock. His rock was added to the memory wall, a long wall of dead, white coral holding a regular pattern of gray rocks.

The following day, currents brought a harsh black grit. It settled slowly, covering everything with a thick layer, like sharp, black snow. It was abrasive, irritating their sensitive skin. Worse yet, it was painful to suck in grit-laden oxygen-water.

Scree gave Orm a mask made from shredded kelp

leaves. "This will help."

"The latest fashion," he joked, putting it on. He turned happy-green. "It really does help!"

Scree made masks for everyone to filter out the grit.

The grit was a worse problem for the reef. Clams and scallops could spit out the grit, but tiny coral polyps could not. The coral would die beneath this dark burden.

Coral was the bedrock of their world, a living rock that grew and repaired itself. It was the stable anchor in a sea of shifting sand, providing homes for myriad life-forms, including octopi. When coral died, the reef wore away and its complex, colorful world vanished with it.

Scree joined the pod, working through each day and into the night. They spread out, carefully dusting grit off the coral reef.

"I'm tired of lifting my arms. It feels like they're turning to lead." Orm gave his arms a dull gray color and let them hang in heavy loops.

Scree laughed. "Mine are so cramped, they're knotting up." She wove all of her eight arms into an elaborate pattern of knots.

Orm nodded approvingly. "That's almost as lacy as a snowflake."

Smiling, Scree turned snow-white. Then she unraveled, stretched each cramped arm, and continued the delicate task of dusting the coral. A very young octopus brought them much-needed snacks. After a brief break, everyone returned to work.

Scree dropped a pinch of food for the glowing reef fish to keep their light on target. "These fish are so beautiful. Tron raved about the strange glowing fish of the abyss. I want to see them some day."

An eight-day later the black snowfall ended. Lava now seeped out slowly, no longer sparking into the sea. There was no more grit, so the corals were safe. Scree collapsed into a trembling heap of cramped, lacerated arms.

Another eight-day passed and the water still tasted of sulfur and odd salts. Fish drifted down like dead leaves, killed by the chemicals. But the sturdy clams and crabs survived. In the far distance, barely visible from her village, white plumes of steam soared to the surface like ghostly kelp.

The distant glow of the volcano became familiar, easily ignored. With homes repaired and plenty of food, the octopi relaxed.

"So many fish have died," Scree said sadly.

"We saved the coral reef," Orm said.

"But the reef looks empty without fish, like a field without butterflies."

The next evening, Scree passed through their quiet, twilit village. Her arms dragged after a long day treating wounded survivors. It was difficult to repair the torn wing fin on the manta ray. Tired and hungry, she didn't notice the deep, unnatural silence of the sea.

A huge, dark shadow moved silently across the sands, slipping over the caves, following behind her.

CHAPTER 8: FORCE OF NATURE

Scree reached her cave and glanced back. The twilit sands had disappeared beneath a huge black shadow. The shadow grew larger, devouring the light, covering the caves like an unnatural shroud. What could it be? She shrank into her cave and froze. Her body instantly camouflaged.

The sea exploded. Long, powerful arms smashed down. Rocks and bodies flew. Two caves were torn apart by a living force of nature. Bright amber lights flashed along its monstrous arms, like lightning. It was a giant squid!

The terrifying creature captured two octopi. They struggled frantically, writhing and twisting, desperate to escape. The giant shook them until they hung limp. Then it swallowed the captives.

Scree watched, stunned, as the living nightmare killed.

Her frozen horror changed to a burning anger. She flowed deeper into her cave and felt around, checking her stores for something to use against the squid. Scree ran arms across her shelves, feeling the bandages, boxes and odd pouches. She stopped at an unusual bottle carved from bright orange garnet, fitted with a tight stopper. This carefully stored container held blue-ringed octopus venom, a deadly nerve poison.

A skilled healer knows that what can heal, can kill. The venom was useful in minute doses to sedate a patient. Larger doses brought paralysis or death.

Scree sucked venom into a long, hollow needle. Then she attached it to the fishing spear that Arak had given her. The shark had been scary, but this was terrifying. Anger barely overcame her terror as she moved stealthily out of her cave.

The monstrous squid suctioned its powerful tentacles onto the rocks of another cave. A violent storm of rubble erupted, and random debris replaced the orderly home. The sea felt unnaturally gritty. Scree watched in horror as a long, snaking arm plucked up another octopus and shook it senseless. Her friend disappeared into its beaked maw.

Trembling with fear and anger, Scree crept ever closer to the living horror. She slid from one cave shadow to another, creeping across the sand, maintaining her camouflage. Finally she was right behind the monster. She focused her mind and stilled her quivering arms.

Scree jetted up and plunged her spear into the back of its huge head.

The monster spun around, but there was nothing to see. It stretched a long, probing arm behind its head, reaching for its tormentor.

Scree held onto her spear for dear life, plunging the needle ever deeper into her foe. She stretched her body flat, almost too thin to feel. She shifted quickly from side to side, trying to avoid the deadly arm as it searched for her.

When would the poison take effect?

A powerful swipe dislodged Scree. The monster turned, swiftly wrapping her in another arm. It pulled her closer. Its huge eyes widened as if surprised by the puny attacker.

Scree was paralyzed, unable to struggle. The powerful arms could easily rip her apart. She would not survive this. The prospect of unavoidable, imminent death was curiously calming. It had been a good life. She would experience what life she had left and die with dignity. Scree looked calmly, defiantly back into its enormous eyes.

The monster continued to stare at Scree, holding her still. It did not shake her. The squid seemed puzzled, perhaps unused to food fighting back quite like this. Then the poison worked. Its eyes went blank. Its arms relaxed their grip.

The squid collapsed in slow motion. Eight thick tentacle arms fell with a jarring thud and lay still, snaking among the ruins. Its huge head fell next, smashing into the reef. Two thin, longer arms fell slowly, like leaves drifting down. Then it did not move.

It was a quiet mountain with saucer eyes.

Orm extracted Scree from the huge arm. "Are you all right? What did you do?"

Scree gathered her thoughts. "I used venom . . . on my spear. We must bind the squid now. It's so huge. I think the paralysis may be temporary. We need lots of ropes. It's powerful."

Orm shuddered. "It *is* powerful, and deadly. Why not kill the monster now?"

"I believe the squid attacked from hunger," Scree said. "Maybe because of the fish kills. It recognized me as un-prey-like before it collapsed."

Orm stiffened his arms. "It killed our friends. It should die."

"Perhaps. It's hard for me to hurt any helpless, intelligent being. And what if more giant squid come? Can we fight many at once? Maybe. But if we can communicate, we might change things."

"You think it can become an envoy for peace," Orm said slowly. "But it's a creature of violence. What if it's a scout and escapes with news of our location? The monster could organize a final attack."

Octopi crept out of their caves. Most watched from a distance, but a few cautiously approached the deathly still monster. Spar twined arms respectfully with Scree. "You are fearless, and you saved us. But your plan would be disastrous for the pod."

Stur spoke up. "Scree got the monster's attention because of her attack. It may only recognize force as an indicator of intelligence. Perhaps it can be reasoned with. But a show of force may be crucial to any communication."

Scree studied her apprentice in silent amazement. He almost never ventured an opinion.

Spar looked from Stur to Scree, as if weighing the risks and possibilities. He turned to Orm. "Could we safely implement Scree's plan?"

Orm thought in stillness. "We need rope, as Scree said, and more dragon spears with poison. A ring of guards should work, with three groups to take turns. "

Spar turned to Stur. "I saw you follow Scree to help. That took courage. Would you fly our skiff to the signal raft and call the dragons?"

A ceremony was held for the octopi killed in the attack, and three more stones were added to the memory wall.

Scree traded Orm's blue-green abalone pearls with the tiny, lethal blue-ringed octopi. They took turns spitting powerful poison into her orange garnet flask. Then Scree attached needles with venom to the dragon spears.

The giant squid looked like a mountain wrapped in ropes. Eight guards stood watch, forming a ring about the prisoner. Each guard tightly clutched a long poison spear.

Scree slowly approached. The squid gnashed its huge, beak-like mouth. It pumped its huge muscles, fighting the ropes yet again. The squid struggled wildly, trying to break a weak cord with sudden stress. There was hatred and anger in its eyes.

Scree remained calm. She made pictures across her body of the destruction in her village. She threatened the monster with her spear. It was a warning: do not attack. We have powerful defenses. Then she slowly lowered her spear to the sand. The monster's eyes followed it down. Scree offered it a huge meal of crabs and oysters. Tantalizing flavors permeated the seawater. But it just eyed her, ignoring the food and testing its bonds.

"It's starving. How can it refuse food?" Scree wondered.

"Fear and anger can be more powerful than hunger," Orm replied.

The giant squid eventually accepted food and gave a

name, Vorm. Gradually, communication improved. Scree used octopus skin pictures and mimes. The squid flashed lights to name things. At last, she understood his fears. Vorm was humiliated by his capture and puzzled by the food offerings. Was he being prepared for a ritual feast? She mimed an emphatic "No."

Scree fed Vorm daily, yet he grew weaker. His limbs twitched and muscles ached.

"Vorm has symptoms of acute mercury and arsenic poisoning. How can this be?" Scree asked.

"I think I know," replied Tarn, their geologist. "My assistant was the last one killed. Tor must have seen the path of destruction and known she was next. I've sifted through the ruins of her cave. The rocks with mercury and arsenic are missing, but the other specimens are still there. Tor must have grabbed the poisonous rocks before she was taken, to retaliate beyond her passing." He shook his head sadly. "She was always quick-thinking."

Scree told Vorm what had happened. "This poisoning has progressed too far and is beyond my ability to treat."

He flashed a complicated pattern of brilliant red and yellow lights, a salute to a worthy opponent who defeated him in battle.

As Vorm lay dying, Scree released his bonds. He spoke of his life in the deep abyss, where adult squid led solitary lives most of the year. "The abyss is my home. I love to surf the strong, deep currents and taste the different streams as they tangle together. It is never truly dark. Life speaks with lights."

Vorm twitched randomly, growing weaker. "Squid gather in large pods each year to choose mates. I mated with Veera every year, but each time I had to win her with my dance. I spun and soared, flashing a rhythm of lights until she joined my dance and we moved as one. Sometimes I was challenged by another male but I never lost."

Scree thought he was finished. Then he flashed more signals. "Veera and I traveled together for a moon after the dance. We battled the giant swordfish. Veera needed their energy for her eggs. Then we would mate and separate until the next fall."

Vorm became still. "I will not see Veera again. This is her name-pattern." He flashed red lights. Scree used her red color cells to mimic the pattern, and this satisfied him. "We do not have caves like you. We live free in the water. We are not much burdened with things. Our experiences . . . our memories . . . all that we truly own is in our mind. But Veera gave me a shell-stone that I carry with me. It was a mating gift. Give it to Veera if you meet her."

Vorm opened a large sucker on his arm and gave Scree a huge, luminous pink pearl. She stared in amazement. It was bigger than her eye and seemed to glow from within. She slipped it into her healer bag.

Vorm requested burial in his home waters, as was their custom. Scree watched sadly as he stilled his mind and accepted death. She helped carry Vorm's body to the edge of the undersea shelf, and released him to his home in the black abyss.

Scree retreated deep into her cave, seeking solitude. She almost never lost a patient. At first she hated Vorm for killing her pod-mates, but he was starving. And then she came to know him. She would miss his wild, free spirit.

Scree remained in her cave and saw no one. Her arms lay in limp coils. Finally, Orm approached and settled next to her. He gave her a large shell full of tender, tantalizing, well-spiced oysters. Scree wondered when she had eaten last. She picked away at the food, gradually feeling a bit better.

"I learned Vorm's language and a little of his customs. He was an intelligent, complicated being. His world is fascinating. And then he died." Scree curled her arms in distress.

Orm twined arms with Scree. "No one could have saved him. But he had the comfort of knowing he would be returned to the deep. You accomplished more than I thought possible, perhaps more than you realize. You succeeded in communicating with Vorm. Now we can converse with a giant squid, if necessary."

Orm smiled and flashed an image of a tiny octopus next to Vorm. "But with such a size difference, introductions are risky."

* * *

Arak glanced down at the waves as he flew to the pod village. Nice, normal waves. One and a half moons had passed since the sea returned to its proper place.

Every dragon remembered the great wave of destruction, but few recalled his warning. Those who did simply thought Arak had a freaky, fortunate dream. So he was still Dreamer to the rowdy young dragons. But not to his friends.

Arak stretched his wings and soared above his three dragon friends, who all glowed golden in the moonlight. Taron and Erinite flew side-by-side with perfectly matching wing strokes, as if they shared one mind. Zarina gazed down as she flew, watching the sparkling sea. They reached the raft together, back-winged and landed lightly.

Scree, Orm and Stur surfaced beside the raft.

The raft lurched, and Arak slid on the damp logs. He barely kept his balance. "The clan's been busy. We lost much to the sea, but we've re-built the guest homes and added many more. Three eight-groups of octopi could attend the next trade festival."

Orm nodded approval. "Good. Many want to come. Those spears you sent were really useful. Tell Kragor that we now know much more about giant squid."

"Stur described the attack when he came for spears, but please tell us the whole story," Arak said.

"Yes!" Taron and Erinite said, together.

Orm told a tale of the squid attack, Scree's defense, and the captive squid. For a master story-teller, he was surprisingly brief. Orm kept glancing at Scree, but she added nothing to the story.

Arak shivered. Orm's skin pictures were the stuff of nightmares! Why did Scree try to save the monster? Wasn't the world better off without it? Giant squid seemed more dangerous than a pack of dweer!

Arak took a closer look at Scree. He might not understand her decision, but she looked ill. Arak worriedly turned to Zarina, but she was already watching his octopus friend.

Zarina sat down next to Scree, letting her legs dangle into the starlit sea. "Scree, you used venom against Vorm in self-defense, but how do you use it to heal?"

The question from a fellow healer seemed to rouse Scree. "I use venom to reduce pain or put a patient to sleep. Choosing the right dose is critical. The proper amount depends on size, age, degree of injury, and type of being. Too much venom is fatal."

Zarina splashed her feet in the sparkling water. "Could you help us determine the right dose for dragons? The trading festival is next moon, but Driana and I would like you to come early."

"We also want more time just to visit," Arak added eagerly. "I now have four octopus capes. We could collect you in two nights and fly you to our shore."

Taron thumped his tail enthusiastically. "You'll be the first to see our new skiffs! These fly as fast as a diving dragon!"

Erinite smiled fondly at Taron.

Arak looked away, desperately wanting such a smile from Zarina. But how? The surrounding sea captured his attention. The moonlit waves had a restless pattern of dark scales with gleaming silver edges.

Arak closed his eyes, remembering his time on the ice floe. It had become a time of peaceful, uncomplicated solitude. There were no decisions to make and no worries about what to say. There was nothing he could do wrong. There was no fear of failure, or ridicule, or rejection.

Zarina's voice broke through his dreaming.

"I found a new herb that might work on octopi," she told Scree encouragingly.

Orm peered anxiously at his quiet mate. "Scree, I think a visit would be good for us."

Scree raised her drooping head and gazed steadily at Orm. "You're right. A visit would be nice." She nodded to Stur. "I saw how much you wanted to fly last time. You should come. And Mir could be the fourth."

Stur turned to Scree with wide eyes. "How did you know . . . I mean, thank you."

Arak sighed. Even the octopi had no trouble with their

90

relationships. Then Zarina turned to him with a smile.

"Thanks for the invitation."

Arak's answering smile almost split his face. He was not going to waste this chance! Taron had advised him to ask questions and listen. "Tell us about your new herb."

Zarina described the tiny golden flowers and how she used them to ease muscle pain. "This even helps my patients who need more copper."

Scree moved closer. "How does it compare to venom?"

"Not as potent. But it's so much easier to collect flowers than venom," Zarina added, laughing.

The cheerful, lively discussion continued until they left. Arak flew near Zarina on their way home, trying to match his wing strokes to hers.

CHAPTER 9: A DANGEROUS GAME

Arak took a deep breath of salty sea air, trying to relax. But he could not stop worrying. First the copper problem and now this! Karoon would be impossible.

Arak tried to drown his worries with busywork. He reached down through the moonlit surf and grabbed a polished white rock. He jerked back as a crab with sharp claws scuttled across his foot. Then he tossed the rock onto his pile of game-stones on the beach.

Arafine paced back and forth nearby, wearing a path in the sand. Arak had never seen his dam so upset. But he was even more worried.

It had been hard enough when Arafine was in charge of resolving disputes. Arafine was careful not to favor her own offspring. So Arak got half the blame for every fight, even though he was only defending himself. He had finally learned to avoid Karoon, since nothing could be worse than those conflict resolution meetings. Until now. Arafine was the new clan leader. What new mischief would Karoon try?

Arak stepped onto the beach, dropped the game-stones into his sack, and asked Arafine, "What's wrong?" He wanted to add, "You're the leader! What could you possibly be worried about?"

Arafine stopped pacing. "Copper deficiencies are already crippling some dragons. We desperately need a new copper mine. And now there's a new, unprecedented danger." She paused, looking out to sea.

"When the undersea volcano erupted, its fumes and odd salts killed many fish. Dragons feed heavily on fish, so this could have been a problem. Fortunately, we have great stores of dried fish, clams, nuts, tubers, and seaweed. But the fish kills are responsible for a more serious problem: starving dweer."

"Why should we care?" Arak said. He'd seen a dweer once, a scaly, wingless, rust-colored beast. It was about one-third his size; only the jagged teeth were impressive.

Arafine replied, "Dweer normally feed on tiny dagurs who eat sea fish. When the fish died the dagurs starved. Now there aren't enough dagurs to feed the dweer. The dweer are hungry and, despite the dangers, they have begun to hunt dragons."

Arak's head was spinning. It was like the game with black and white stones on a checkered log. One jump led to the next. But this was a dangerous game. "Dweer were always afraid of us. What's changed?"

"There's a clever new leader and he's uniting all the separate packs. The combined pack has many more dweer than the clan has dragons. Normally, our natural defenses would be enough. But the united dweer could challenge the dragons."

Arak straightened his wings and gave her his full attention. "What do you plan to do about this?"

Arafine snapped her tail. "I need to change the rules and the clan won't like that. Spar doesn't realize how easy he has it. Octopi are vulnerable from the moment they hatch, and only a few survive. Most octopi appreciate a safe village and willingly accept Spar's authority."

Except for Scree, Arak thought. She must be part dragon.

93

"But dragon eggs are rare, and dragonlets are pampered from the day they hatch. Dragons are at the top of the food chain. They feel all-powerful and don't easily accept authority." Arafine sighed. "Dragons are so different from octopi. It's a real challenge to manage the clan."

Arak and Arafine flew to the clan meeting. As leader, Arafine took her place in the center of the circle. She proposed several defense measures but most were rejected.

The following evening, Arak again took his place in the clan circle. The central fire had no festive blue-green flames, just the traditional orange and yellow from burning logs. Another meeting and even the fire was serious.

Arafine raised her wings and the clan grew silent. Her voice was strong and persuasive. "The dweer pose a serious threat. We need to be prepared. There must be at least three dragons in any group, to protect against ambush. There should be no solo journeys. Perimeter guards would be useful. And we must triple the guard on our dragonlets."

"We need our time alone. Dweer are small and they can't fly or flame. Why should we be afraid? We are dragons!" challenged a young dragon-lord.

"Dweer are wily and tireless hunters, and they outnumber us," Arafine responded. "Also . . ."

Karana, their former leader, suddenly landed inside the circle. "A dragonlet is missing from the crèche. She may be in danger."

Arafine assigned four dragons to search.

Arak was proud to be chosen. He left immediately with Kragor, Taron and Rikor. They flew swiftly to the crèche. Then they separated into pairs and headed downhill in the two most likely directions.

A dragonlet screamed! Arak tore through the skies.

Her piercing, frantic cries made his scales crawl. He cleared the trees and found her in a meadow. She was completely surrounded. There was nowhere to flee. The dweer held their positions, quivering with anticipation. The leader signaled and the pack attacked as one, racing to their meal.

Arak and Kragor reached the dragonlet just as the eager predators closed in. Three dweer clamped their jaws on her legs, slightly hampered by the tough dragon hide. She reared back. Another dove for the softer skin of her exposed belly.

Arak flamed the closest dweer while Kragor grabbed Dorali's wings with his claws, desperately attempting to lift her above the fray. Arak smelled an awful mix of dragon blood and the stench of burned dweer. He grasped Dorali's tail and together they lifted the bloody dragonlet off the battleground.

Hungry dweer ripped slices from her body before she rose beyond their range. Kragor's claws tore holes in her wings as they flew, but there was no other option. Dorali was too young to fly, and they could not fight so many dweer.

Torn and bleeding, Dorali hung limp from four sets of claws. Arak pushed beyond his limits to carry such a burden. His long, trembling wings grabbed the air with ragged strokes. Arak and Kragor landed at the clinic, setting down carefully despite their exhaustion.

Arak slumped to the ground while Driana extracted Kragor's claws from the dragonlet's wings.

"Get Scree," Driana told Arak. "Ask her to bring her bag and the venom. We need all the help we can get."

Arak heaved upright and headed for the shore to signal

Scree from her guest home.

"Taron," Driana called out as he landed. "Fill this kettle with water and boil it."

Dorali began to moan just as Scree arrived, bringing the requested items and her abundant supply of kelp bandages.

"I can sedate her while we put her back together," Scree offered.

Driana nodded. "That would be helpful."

Zarina unwound the rolls of bandages. Driana held the wound edges together with her claws. Scree's many arms worked efficiently to wind bandages around Dorali's gaping wounds. She always included pieces of iodine-rich seaweed to prevent infection.

Arak lay limp on the sand, watching the healers as they worked on Dorali. Scree had used those odd bits of seaweed when she fixed his injuries. His gaze shifted to Zarina. She looked intensely energized and worn out at the same time.

"Taron, they must be getting tired, and I still feel like a flopping fish. Could you get some red root drinks and snacks?"

Zarina flashed a grateful smile to Arak and continued her work.

News of the attack traveled lightning fast and all the dragons were eager to help, quickly assembling food. Taron soon returned with another dragon, each carrying a huge basket. But the healers ignored the food and continued their work. They had reached a critical point and were completely absorbed, oblivious to the tantalizing aromas that swirled around them.

Dorali was soon completely covered in bandages.

Scree checked her pulse. "She'll wake before moonrise, and then need painkillers. What do you use?"

"We have several, but the most potent is brewed from flame flowers. That would be my choice, with such extensive injuries," Driana replied. "Then she'll need warm fish broth with lots of rosemary, onions and garlic, to help cleanse the blood."

Arak approached. "If you've done all you can, you should feed."

Driana looked up, finally noticing a world beyond her patient. "I think I am hungry," she said, surprised. "Thank you all for your help rescuing Dorali. Scree, this was a real challenge. We really needed you."

Scree looked Driana straight in the eyes and bowed. "I was honored to help, my friend."

Silence descended as they fed.

Zarina worriedly tucked more blankets around the sedated dragonlet. Then she asked the question everyone was afraid to ask. "Will she live?"

Driana studied their young patient silently. "I hope so. We've done all we can, for now. She's young, still growing. That will help."

Arak carried the teapot to Zarina and noted her limp wings. She looked even more exhausted than he felt. "Are you all right?"

Zarina held out her mug while Arak poured. She took a sip, tried to smile, and sighed. "I was the youngest dragonlet ever chosen to be trained as healer, and I love my work. But this is so intense! Even with three of us working on Dorali, I'm drained. How can I possibly handle being clan healer? And a healer works most of her life, seeking one trainee to replace her."

97

She lowered her voice. "Healing is Driana's life. She has no mate. But I'm not sure what I want. I might like a dragonlet of my own someday."

Arak put a comforting wing around Zarina. Then he sharpened his claws in the sand, considering. Was it possible to be both a healer and mated? His thoughts turned to Scree. She had a mate.

Arak asked Scree, "What's it like to be a pod healer?"

"Octopi are sturdy, so healers are seldom over-worked. Arm cuts and torn suckers are the most common problem. I just wrap them in kelp bandages with lots of iodine-rich seaweed, and they'll usually heal themselves."

Scree stretched her arms. "I like being a healer. It gives me an excuse to go off on my own to find medicinal supplies. Most octopi had enough solitude during the two years before they found the pod. But I still need the freedom to explore alone."

Driana joined them. "A dragon healer has less freedom. We can't leave on long journeys because we're needed too often, but I plan to change that. Zarina and I should train several healers. We could take turns, and work together on serious injuries or with many sick dragons."

Zarina stared wide-eyed at her mentor, who returned a knowing smile.

Arak grinned at Zarina as he refilled her mug. "That must be a relief."

She took a long drink of tea and a true smile spread across her face. "I've been so worried. I feel as though I've been under a crushing boulder, and it just turned to snow and melted away."

The following evening, Arak settled near the crackling fire and waited for the meeting to begin. Most of the clan members were present, whispering quietly, as solemn as the gray smoke.

Dorali's dam jumped up, wings snapping, glaring at Arafine. "How could you let this happen?"

Arafine moved forward to speak, but the former leader raised her wings high and took command.

Karana spoke with an icy edge to her voice. "Dorali is still alive because Arafine insisted on continual trance-mind watches. We are fortunate for her foresight. She asked for greater measures but few saw the need." Karana paused, looking from dragon to dragon. Many looked away from her sharp gaze.

Arafine rustled her wings and her eyes flashed angry sparks.

Arak blinked in surprise. Karana's interfering support actually undermined Arafine's authority as new leader.

Arafine swept her wings up and reclaimed her command. "Thank you, Karana. We do need more measures to protect against the dweer." She turned to the angry dragon. "Dorali should recover. She was fortunate to have three healers to attend her." Arafine paused. "I should have tripled the guard on dragonlets but I sought consensus, as is our way."

Arafine turned in a slow circle, meeting the eyes of each clan member. "The real problem is the dweer. Are there any objections to my proposals?"

Arak was not surprised when the new rules passed, unanimously.

Karoon cried loudly, "Destroy the dweer!"

"Karoon is right! Finish it now!"

Many young dragon-lords took up the cry.

Arafine waited for the furor to die down. "I, too, am

angered by the attack on Dorali. However, I'm not sure we could, or should, destroy the dweer. They naturally control the dagur population and may have other uses. But this new leader has changed them. The dweer must learn to fear us again."

Karoon demanded, "Attack now!"

Arafine raised her wings for silence. "We need more information first. How can we organize an attack so that no dragon is injured? If any are wounded, or killed, the cost is too high."

"There is always risk. To do nothing is risky," Karoon countered, now sounding calm and reasonable. Arak knew that voice. Karoon had used it in their conflict sessions, cleverly deflecting blame.

Arafine gave Karoon a stern look. "We will take the time we need to develop a plan that minimizes risk." There was steel in her voice.

Arak flicked his tail and smiled. It was a real pleasure to see his dam stand firm in the face of Karoon's demands.

Zarina said, "The venom that Scree has can sedate or kill any creature. She used it on the giant squid. We could trade for venom and use it on fishing spears to attack the dweer."

Arafine nodded. "That's good, and it keeps our flame for back-up. We should use a venom dose that's safe for dragons, to protect against bad throws."

Arak spoke up. "Dweer silently surround their prey and attack at the same time on a signal."

"A surprise attack. That would help." Arafine turned to Rikor. "You have a gift for strategy. I need a battle plan that leaves a third of the dweer alive, for their natural roles. But we must kill their leader."

Karoon jumped to his feet, eyes flashing. "Why leave any dweer alive? Our world would be fine without them!"

"Karoon, you speak out of turn. But consider this. It is easier to kill than to restore life. We know little of the dweer, mostly the negatives. Dweer hunt the dagur, which are normally so abundant that they could over-run this land. What would take the place of the dweer? If we're not careful, we might solve one problem while creating new problems we cannot yet imagine."

* * *

Scree was half asleep, tasting the air with her arms. Mingled odors of kelp bandages, torn flesh and brewed sedative permeated the dragon clinic. She opened her eyes and automatically reached over, checking the dragonlet. Dorali was still alive. Scree felt such intense relief that it was almost painful. She had spent the night next to her, checking often, unwilling to lose another patient.

After that night, Dorali improved daily. Her wounds were healing well, and a numbing flame flower brew took away the pain. But she still lay curled on her side, wings limp. There was no sparkle in her eyes and she barely responded to questions.

Scree looked worriedly at Driana, who snapped her tail in frustration. "I prefer a nuisance to a shadow. Zarina, do you have any suggestions on how to reach Dorali?"

"A storyteller could help, and she'd love your unusual pictures, Scree." Zarina stretched her wings, stared, and gave a startled cry. "Dorali's a rising two-year! She wants to fly. Is that still possible?"

Driana answered carefully. "Her wings have many holes and tears from Kragor's claws. He saved her life with his quick thinking and I know he hated inflicting more damage. The wings should heal, though more slowly than her body. But, eventually, she should have proper dragon wings and learn to fly."

"She needs to know, to have that dream alive."

Everyone could see the spark ignite in Dorali's eyes when she learned that she would still be able to fly.

Zarina tilted her head, considering. "Scree, this is a challenge even for us, and Driana's an expert. How in blue lightning did *you* learn to heal dragons?"

Scree gave a wry smile. "Maybe I was bored?"

Scree shifted to a more comfortable position. "I was young, barely an adult, when I became the pod healer. I'd already mastered octopus healing, so I moved on to fish. This seemed reasonable since fish are honored in our legends. And bones are so *fascinating*. We don't have any. I learned new ways to communicate. I changed the shape of my body and copied the movements of fish. I watched carefully until I understood their language of postures, wriggles, and touch."

Scree noticed that Orm was watching, too.

"I studied cleaner stations, where fish hold still while smaller fish or shrimp remove parasites. I learned to direct the movements of a fish by touching certain spots in its mouth with a thin stick. I could calm a fish by stroking the sensitive lateral line scales along its sides."

Scree slipped off her log seat into the stream and became a fish. She molded her head to a point, merging her arms behind. She bent four arms to mimic the top, bottom, and side fins of a fish. Four more arms made the rest of the body and tail fin. A pattern of gray fish scales covered her, and a mouth groove appeared at the tip of her head. Scree demonstrated typical fish movements. Then she flowed back to her seat.

Zarina wore a stunned expression. "You really looked like a fish."

"What I become, I can understand. At first I healed small, colorful reef fish. Then I found a stingray with a badly torn wing fin. I tried my usual approach and it seemed to accept my offer. It followed me to an open area near the pod. Spar saw the fish and his arms went rigid. He charged toward us and ordered me to send the stingray away, immediately."

Scree's arms stiffened automatically at this memory.

"When Spar charged, the injured fish panicked and fled toward the pod. Spar waved his arms to scare it away and was stung. This would *not* have happened if he had trusted me, and given the stingray the space it needed. I don't think Spar will ever understand."

Scree relaxed her arms, letting them trail in the water. "I found a turtle with serious injuries from a shark attack. She was desperately ill and readily accepted my help. I repaired Tara's shell and learned new ways to heal. I understood the role of nutrition, and Orm taught me more about trace metals from his experiments. So I was prepared when Arak crashed, even though I'd never seen a dragon."

"You were born to heal," Driana said. "And it took courage to face a dragon."

Scree laughed. "Actually, I was terrified. I wanted to flee. But I couldn't let the golden creature suffer when I knew I could help."

Orm flowed onto a seat next to Scree. "I never heard the whole story about the stingray. Now I understand why you didn't want to tell Spar about Arak."

Scree nodded. "Spar is a good leader. But sometimes

he sees only what he expects to see. He sees danger, not opportunity."

Zarina finished rolling up a bandage, tied it off, and put it in a supply box. "Perhaps friendship with dragons will widen his eyes."

"The sight of a dragon would widen any eyes," Orm said, and they all laughed.

A five-day later, Dorali wore fewer bandages. Scree watched as Zarina developed a new skill of encouraging scales to grow across wounds. She pulsed the barest amount of energy through her claws at just the right frequency.

Driana nodded approval. "That's more complicated than helping bones grow together. I hope these skills won't be needed when the dragons fight the dweer."

* * *

Dark, spiky shapes moved against the blood-red sunrise. The best marks-dragons were armed, assembled and waiting. Arak made his way to the front of the dragons just as the scouts landed in a flurry of wings, reporting the dweer location in a large meadow.

Arak edged closer, waiting for Rikor's orders.

"We'll approach from downwind, encircle the pack, and attack from the sky. The dweer leader is our most important target. He's larger, darker, and the pack obeys his signals." Rikor looked from dragon to dragon. "Attack on my signal, use your spears wisely, and make clean kills." He pumped his fist, snapped his wings wide and shot into the sky.

Arak followed in a heartbeat, barely able to see through the surge of pumping wings and swirling dust. The sky cleared as they rose higher. A roil of emotions churned in his gut: excitement, fear, worry, doubt.

Arak caught a thermal and settled into his own flight path, thinking. The relatively thin, scaly hides of the dweer should be easily pierced by a fishing spear. Each spear point was coated with just enough venom to put a dragon to sleep, but this amount would quickly kill a dweer. So suffering should be minimal. Few dragons were concerned with dweer suffering, but this mattered greatly to Scree.

Arak had wondered if she would provide the venom. Although Scree understood defense, she much preferred diplomacy over this brutal plan. "Civilized creatures should seek civilized solutions to conflicts," she said. Arafine had replied that this danger was too great. Dragons would only kill enough dweer to reduce the threat, and venom would kill without pain. Scree reluctantly agreed to help.

All too soon the lush meadow lay below, and sweet scents of sun-warmed grasses washed over Arak. It seemed far too lovely for a battlefield.

Rikor gave the signal to attack. The dragons surged forward, staying safely above the range of a leaping dweer.

Below, a dark, brawny dweer snapped its head around. They were spotted. The dweer leader gave a high-pitched howl and two short, low grunts. The pack responded instantly, retreating toward their narrow underground warrens.

Spear after spear rained down harmlessly from the sky. Few dweer were hit. They ran jagged, twisting paths, presenting difficult targets. Many were escaping into their warrens.

Arak had speared sturgeon while standing on the river bank, and he'd practiced throwing spears at moving targets while flying. But it became painfully clear that even throwing spears at a dragged skin could not compare with the challenge of trying to hit a motivated, fleeing dweer.

Arak saw Karoon dip from the sky and hover momentarily as he quickly threw a spear. He nicked his target and the dweer vanished into thicker cover. He chose another dweer and threw more carefully. The beast jerked and pitched forward as the spear hit home.

Karoon grinned and brayed his success.

Arak hovered, uncertain. These creatures were nothing like the sturgeons that dragons routinely hunted. Dweer were swift, wily, and undeniably intelligent. His eyes swept the meadow. Targets were disappearing at a rapid rate. If he didn't hurry, they'd all be gone before he even tried. Still, he took the time to carefully select a likely target.

Arak chose a lone dweer that had darted from the thin, scraggly brush, far from their caves. That one should be easy to get. He readied his spear, considering both the wind and the dweer path, and threw slightly ahead of his moving target.

The dweer fell, arched its back, and became as still as ice. It would never run again.

Arak snapped his tail with pride. Then, as he hovered above the carcass, his wings shook. He had never killed except for food. His brief joy vanished as swiftly as the sun slipping behind dark clouds. But he'd accepted this task and grimly chose another target.

Arak spotted a dweer lurking in the brush. He flew lower and flushed it from hiding, following from above as it ran a fairly predictable course. Again he aimed ahead. His second target jerked sideways and sprawled in the grass.

Karoon swerved in front of Arak, hurling his third and

last spear. He missed. Karoon stormed away, clipping Arak's wing just as he was regaining his balance.

Arak tumbled down. An angry dweer leapt high. Wickedly sharp teeth scraped his belly, drawing blood. Shocked, he fell further. The dweer caught his wing. Jerked from the sky, he smashed onto the dweer. They were both winded.

Arak rolled off the dweer and thrust his spear into it. The dweer faltered and fell.

A new dweer joined the attack and sprang for his throat. Arak reared back. He gripped the spear that he'd recovered and thrust it into the dweer. It stumbled back.

A third came from behind and clamped powerful jaws on his leg. Pain tore through Arak's leg as he tried to twist away from the dweer. But this one held fast. Arak arched his long neck and breathed flames. The dweer flinched and held on. He flamed again and the dweer loosened its grip. Arak kicked free.

A fourth dweer sprang from the bushes. He was a magnet for angry dweer! Arak leapt clumsily into the sky, barely in time. But his wings beat off-kilter and he couldn't catch the wind. The dweer raked him with razor claws. Desperately, Arak willed his wings to work together. He found his balance and swooped higher.

Arak looked down from safety. Blood trickled across his belly and his leg throbbed with pain. Despite these injuries, he felt no anger toward the dweer. They were only defending themselves. But Karoon was another matter.

The dweer leader zigged from behind a boulder. He was still alive. Three dragons pursued. Spears flew but only one struck the target, and it was a glancing blow. The leader was skilled at running an unpredictable pattern, veering rapidly left or right. He dove into a crevice.

The tunnel entrance was too small for dragons, and dweer had long ago learned the limits of dragon flame. Along with the leader, the survivors had gone to ground.

Two piercing whistles split the air. The dragons stowed any unused spears and flew to Rikor. The battle was over.

It was an eerie sight, a meadow full of dweer seemingly asleep in unnatural positions. Arak landed between two dead dweer. Fat black flies already crawled over the stiff, gaunt carcasses. Blank eyes stared at him, accusingly. He turned away. His injuries ached fiercely but he would soon recover. These dweer would not.

Arak stopped the bleeding with herbs from his pack and wrapped his ankle for support. He'd learned a few useful tricks from Zarina.

Karoon landed. His gaze slid slowly from Arak's injured chest to his foot. He grinned. "Clumsy again? Too slow for a dweer?"

Another insult, on top of years of insults. Arak snapped back, "There were four. And I was on the ground, thanks to your wing-clipping." Arak flexed his claws, measuring his opponent. He'd grown and was now almost as big as Karoon. He was injured, but anger would give him strength. He'd just fought four dweer, alone. He could fight one dragon.

Karoon looked surprised. Then his eyes turned battle-bright and he flared his wings. He crouched and snarled.

Arak tracked his opponent as they began circling. He searched for an opening, ready to spring.

"Recover the spears," Rikor ordered. "All must be accounted for. Dweer might find a way to use these against us. Meet back here."

Rikor's voice was a murmur, lost in the raging sea of anger that filled Arak's head.

"Arak! Karoon!"

The whip-like voice broke through Arak's battle-lust. He stopped circling.

"We came to fight *dweer*. Now collect the spears."

Arak turned to obey.

"Arak, those spear markers were a good idea," Rikor added, giving him a friendly shoulder clout.

Arak bowed his thanks, unable to speak. The chance to fight back had slipped away. Next time, nothing would stop him. Following orders, he pulled a spear from a dweer. Then he smiled with satisfaction. Adding red leather ribbons to the spears really was a good idea, since they were easy to spot.

Arak returned to base with Rikor. Arafine studied Arak's injuries but, mercifully, said nothing.

"The dweer made difficult targets and most escaped to their underground tunnels. But our injuries were minor and all spears were recovered. It seems that battles are easier to plan than to execute," Rikor reported.

Arafine nodded agreement. "Plans seldom unfold as expected."

"Sad but true. The dweer leader seems very intelligent, so he'll probably avoid us now. It could even prove useful that he survived," Rikor said.

The following day, Arak flew over the battlefield with Kragor and Rikor. The dead bodies had all disappeared. The meadow was empty, as if nothing had ever happened. They landed and searched among the bushes, finding bloodstains but nothing else.

Rikor shrugged his wings, baffled. "I expected torn

carcasses, some shark-like cannibalism. How much has prejudice influenced our knowledge of the dweer?"

"The dweer are too bold, but they're starving. If they had not attacked Dorali, I might pity them," Kragor replied.

Arak was silent. Starvation had forced the dweer into this unusual conflict with the clan. But their leader was clever, and his quick response had countered much of their planning. Did he have a name? What did they know of dweer customs? Was Scree right?

The old, uneasy truce between dweer and dragon returned. The battle was considered a success, but Arak found the slaughter disturbing. He remembered the dragonlet Scree helped save, using the venom as an anesthetic. She'd found a better use for the venom.

Arak found Scree at the dragon clinic, talking with Driana. He waited while they discussed a treatment plan for Dorali. This talk of bandages and soothing creams contrasted oddly with his memories of the battle. He sat on the shore with his feet in the surf, studying the placid waves, remembering dangerous storm surges. The life-like sea seemed to be breathing, shifting in and sucking away. It could be gentle or deadly. Like a dragon. Or a dweer?

Driana left and Arak asked Scree, "Why did you save the giant squid?"

Scree settled herself on a closer seat and gave him her full attention. "It was helpless, desperately hungry, and seemed intelligent. I could not bring myself to kill it. Also, I could learn more about Vorm and his kind if we conversed, and it never hurts to learn." She gave a rueful smile. "It was not a popular view. Why do you ask?"

Arak was still for a moment, gathering his thoughts. "My dreams are invaded by a field of dead dweer. The battle was not what I expected, and now I question our judgment. I wonder if we could have found another way."

Scree nodded approvingly. "Viewpoint is everything. You can only see what you are prepared to see. Force can be necessary in dealing with a powerful enemy like the giant squid. But communication is always the key."

She broke off, watching a leaf swirl in the surf. Arak followed her gaze. The leaf found another current and whirled away behind a bend in the shore.

Scree smiled. "Who knows where that leaf will go? Who knows where a thought will lead?" There was a far-away look in her eyes. "Change is seldom easy. But the ripples from a single stone can cross the sea."

CHAPTER 10: LEGENDS

Arak stepped into the sea, sinking his claws into the cool, wet sand. Froth eddied about his ankles. He stood next to Kragor in the surf, waiting. Orm relaxed nearby, his arms drifting back and forth with the waves like kelp leaves.

The first full moon of spring lit the waves. What had Scree said? Ripples of change? That was happening now. Octopi would soon arrive for the second trading festival. This was a bright spot for the clan, a vacation of sorts from their frantic search for copper.

Kragor said to Orm, "Show me your garden."

Orm flashed a detailed image across his skin. The seafloor outside his cave was paved with white clam shells and smooth gray stones, in a geometric design of overlapping waves. A living border continued this pattern. Interlocking circles of purple sea fans were filled with gold and purple-green seaweeds.

"Your garden is truly artistic," Kragor said.

Arak smiled; that was Kragor's highest praise. He flicked his tongue, automatically cleaning the cloudy spots of dried sea spray off his bright scales. The salt whetted his appetite for the evening feast.

That night, Arak lit one of the huge fires by the shore while octopi arranged themselves on the log sea seats. Making a great fire was an art. Salt-soaked pinecones were frequently tossed in, accenting the orange flames with tongues of blue-green fire. He added ground metals for rainbow flames and used special woods and oils to scent the fire.

Smoke flavored the air. Roasting nuts, tubers, crab claws and fish added tantalizing aromas, while small, colorful ears of wild corn exploded into puffy treats. Food was plentiful, and spiced red-root tea flowed freely.

All was well, except for the looming copper disaster.

Search teams had found no new mines. Dragon claws grew weaker and scales lost their sparkle. Strange aches and pains invaded their bodies.

Zarina had told him the horrors to come, if no more copper was found: their scales would fade to a dull orange, muscles would cramp and wither away, and flying would become impossible. Arak shook the terrible images from his mind. Tonight he would simply enjoy the festival.

Arafine raised her wings for silence. "It's time for story-telling."

"Tell us the story of the ice dragons!" begged a dragonlet.

"Yes!" said another.

"We want to hear the legend!"

Arak thumped his tail. This was his favorite legend! And it was perfect for the new sign language, which used gestures from both dragons and octopi. There was a certain pride in using new expressions. Dragons spoke of changing your colors when considering a new idea. Octopi bent two arms like folded wings to give in and accept that the other being was right. Story-telling was more complex and beautiful.

Kragor stepped forward. He swept his wings upwards and all voices stilled.

"This is the legend of the ice dragons," Kragor said, in a deep, dramatic voice. He wove sign language between his gestures. "Long ago, our world was white. The sun was dim and often hidden by snowstorms. Ice covered the land."

Kragor pointed a wing toward the ice edge, which was ghostly white in the pale moonlight.

"The ice dragons had large, snowy wings. Their scales were white moonstones edged with glittering diamonds. They were made from snowy moonbeams and icy starlight. Ice dragons were huge, with twice my wingspan."

Kragor flexed his wings to their fullest. Arak joined him, wing-to-wing, to show the immense size.

"They lived on the ice and dove into the sea for fish. These dragons did not use fire or talk mind-to-mind. But they did play catch with lightning, as we do. And ice dragons could fly further and higher than we can, far above the storms. Then the world changed. The sun became hotter and the ice began to melt. Glacier edges moved in from the sea and golden beaches were seen for the first time."

Kragor paused dramatically, his eyes sweeping over the beach. "Their white world had color. Some dragons moved off the ice to see the new sand. The sun caught these ice dragons and turned them to gold."

Kragor gathered a claw-full of sand and held it high, letting it sift through his claws. The sand and his scales gleamed golden in the firelight.

"Other dragons stayed on the ice. They worked together, rolling huge rocks to the edge of the ice. They pushed the boulders off, building an immense wall to protect the ice from the sun. But the sun was too strong. Most of the ice is now gone and the ice dragons are gone. Some say they died with the ice. But stories passed down beyond memory claim that they flew very high and found a new land of ice, where they still live."

Kragor bowed to his audience.

Dragons enthusiastically thumped their tails and octopi turned exotic colors to applaud. There were copper arms with blue swirls, pink arms with green diamonds, violet arms with yellow dots, and more. Octopi also used their arms to sign words of praise.

Scree flashed gold to catch Kragor's attention. "No one has seen the ice dragons since?"

"No. But a jumbled wall of gray boulders can still be seen far to the south. The solid bedrock in that region is different, pink with black specks. Something moved those huge gray rocks."

Orm asked, "Why didn't the ice dragons use fire?"

"I don't think they knew they could," Kragor replied. "Also, there was little to burn, and they liked raw fish. Flying is as natural to us as water-pulsing is to you, but fire was a discovery."

"How?"

"Another legend tells of a dragon who enjoyed making sparks with his claws. He could even start fire in dry grass. One day he spit oil into a rock hollow and lit a fire with his sparks. Then he learned to spit an oil stream and light it. He taught all the dragons. Our flames could make hot tea and roasted nuts. And now we had a new weapon. Dagur and dweer had moved into our area, and dweer can be deadly."

Kragor bowed once more and moved back to his place by the fire.

Arafine raised her wings. "Who should be next?"

Zarina stood up. "We want an octopus legend!"

There were cries and gestures of encouragement. What would a pod legend be like?

Orm rippled off his seat, grasping a small, sturdy sack made from the flexible purple skeletons of sea fans. He climbed the damp log ramp to a curved, water-filled platform. It was shallow, a few feet above the beach, and visible to everyone. He raised two arms high and a profound silence settled over the clan.

"This is the legend of Sorm, the first octopus." Orm spoke like a dancer, with eloquent gestures.

Adults translated quietly for the youngest dragons.

"Our mother, the Moon, ruled the seas and created the tides. But she was lonely. She wanted a child. So she gathered rich mud from the bottom of the sea and formed a round head like the moon. Then she made two arms for each of her four moon phases."

Orm closed his eyes. His head turned white like a full moon. He twisted each pair of arms together, until they seemed like four. Then he lifted his arms high and unraveled the pairs into eight octopus arms.

"She showered her child with moonlight, and his arms danced with life! But he could not see. So she gave him eyes."

Orm opened his eyes.

"When he saw his beautiful mother, he bowed before her. The Moon was pleased and gave him more ways to know her world. He could taste subtle flavors and feel the most delicate touch. He could feel-hear the beating sounds in the sea. His mind could remember and imagine. She named him Sorm.

"'What must I do?' he asked.

"'You must prove yourself by performing four tasks, one for each of my phases. Then you will be worthy to be called my child and I will give you a home in the sea,' the Moon replied.

"Sorm's first task was to find a shell that swims. He searched the sea. There were clams that hopped, conchs that crawled, and oysters that couldn't move at all. Finally he saw a flock of scallops, using their two shells like wings, flying in spurts through the water. The Moon was pleased, and shell-food became our first food."

Orm used his arms to fly the scallop shells.

"The second task was to find a ball of sky living in the sea. Sorm pulsed to the surface and caught pieces of sky in his suckers, dragging them under. They tasted and felt like nothing. Sorm released them, watching as silver bubbles flew to the surface like living creatures.

"He rose again, filling all his suckers with sky. This time he was held at the surface, floating. Sorm released the sky. Now he had a clue. Still, Sorm searched long before he found sky living inside seaweed floats. Seaweed became our second food.

"The third task was more difficult: 'Create my image on your skin and of your skin, to show you are my child.' Sorm made dyes but they quickly faded, and were not truly of his skin. He could change his skin colors to match

117

almost anything, but it happened without thought. Then he made a dark circle on white sand and concentrated when his body naturally made a circle. He tried and tried, until he could make the full moon circle at any time. The Moon approved, and Sorm learned a new way to communicate."

Orm imaged a simple moon circle on his body, turning so all could see.

"The fourth and last task was the most difficult: 'Find the most beautiful stone.' It seemed easy, for there were many lovely stones in the sea. But the Moon lived in the sky.

"Sorm searched far and wide for a stone that would please her. Red coral was a living jewel the color of a sunset sky. Black garnet was a rare, glittering gem like a star-studded sky. Coral agate looked like a storm cloud, with lightning colors running through its lumpy white surface. Sorm trembled with excitement when he found a white marble ball in a sea-flooded cave. It looked just like the full Moon. But it was dull."

Orm raised four arms. He held a branch of polished red coral, sparkling black garnet, colorful coral agate and a white cave pearl. These exotic, rarely-seen stones caught the eye. Orm loved this legend and had decided as a young octopus to find each stone.

"Almost two years had passed. Sorm yearned to complete his task, to earn his place in his mother's heart and in the sea. He was tired of traveling. He wanted a home. But he was afraid to bring the wrong stone. No stone seemed quite perfect enough for the Moon.

"As Sorm pulsed through the water, searching, a flash of silver caught his eye. A fish thrashed, struggling desperately, its fin caught in the seam of a large oyster shell. 'Help me!'

"Sorm grabbed the shell and pried it apart, just a little. The fish swam free. But it did not leave, even though it feared the octopus. 'You saved me. I am in your debt. How can I help you?' asked the fish.

"'I must find the most beautiful stone for the Moon,' Sorm replied.

"'Open this shell, and you will find what you seek,' said the grateful fish.

"Sorm opened the oyster and found a large, round, gleaming white pearl. This was the perfect stone! It looked just like the Moon. Sorm gave her the pearl.

"'You are indeed the child of my heart,' the Moon said, and gave him a beautiful cave in the sea."

Orm illustrated the legend with vivid scenes that moved across his body. Dragon eyes glittered in the firelight, and there was not a sound to be heard.

"Because the fish helped, octopi do not eat fish. And even today, all newly-hatched octopi must prove themselves. They leave home and live a dangerous life on the waves for almost two years before they return. Survivors are welcomed home, just as Sorm was. Octopi celebrate our mother with the New Moon Festival. We feast, to remind her to grow full and bright again. We dance with pearls to celebrate her beauty."

Orm lifted a huge white pearl above his rapt audience as he ended the story. It shone like white fire against his red-brown skin. Then he danced with the pearl. It slid down one flexible arm and was flipped to the next, caught and flung in a pattern. Orm had practiced in the air, since a pearl moved differently underwater.

The fire crackled. All eyes were fixed on Orm. He

tossed the ball incredibly high, whirling like a top beneath it. He caught the pearl, paused, and bowed.

Arafine spoke into the silence. "That was exceptional, Orm."

The dragons thumped their tails. Octopi wove their colorful arms in exuberant patterns to show their pride. Orm bowed again in all directions and flowed down the ramp, returning to his shore seat.

"Now we'll let the fires burn down, but stay as long as you wish," Arafine said.

Pod and clan relaxed under the stars, chatting companionably into the night. Finally, tired octopi bid good night to drowsy dragons and drifted down to their undersea caves.

The following evening, trading began in earnest. Intriguing new items were given as gifts, with hopes for future trade. Arafine handed Spar a sack of dried fish swim bladders. "These floats will lighten the loads that the pod tows home."

Spar gave Arafine a large packet of brown seaweed. "Boil this to thicken those magnificent dragon sauces." He reached into his sack and held out another bag filled with rare, perfect shells. "And these are to decorate nest bowls."

Arafine snapped her tail with delight as she rifled through the bright red, purple, and orange scallop shells.

Arak bargained with Orm and Scree, who wanted the eight new skiffs for the pod. These had a new design, and could really fly! He traded the skiffs for pearls, venom and dried seaweed.

Kragor gave Orm a box carved from the heart of yellow pine, a sturdy, dense wood that could withstand the sea. It was filled with a fungus that glowed yellow, to light the skiff masts at night so the pod could stay together. Orm twirled his arms excitedly. "This is great! The journey home is long, and I fear Scree has plans to travel even further."

Kragor asked eagerly, "Did you bring the tunicates?"

Orm hefted a mesh bag that glowed from within. "These should be enough for a good pattern. I'll help you place them."

Together they created a tunicate tapestry below low tide. Kragor poked his head under the sea to enjoy the full effect of bright colors glowing in the dark.

Arak admired the sea garden, which was truly beautiful. Even more remarkable was the friendship between his sire and Orm. They could be nest-mates.

* * *

That night, Orm helped Scree rig the new skiffs. Eight pod members climbed aboard, eager to skiff-fly. They would also learn to navigate by the stars.

"I thought the tunicate sky I made for your cave would be the end of my star studies," Orm said.

"It was an excellent start," Scree replied. She pointed to the skiff-fliers, who were busy practicing their skills. "Look how well they're doing."

Stur dropped his paddle overboard and circled to pick it up, a test to prove mastery of wing and winds. Mir swooped by in her skiff and stealthily grabbed the paddle. Stur looked alarmed when he couldn't find it. Mir wriggled with silent laughter and tossed him the missing paddle.

"Well enough to tease each other," Orm acknowledged. "But do they know enough for a safe trip home?"

Scree's eyes twinkled. "At least we'll be safe from

sharks." She fidgeted nervously. "Orm, we now have eight skiffs, plus one to leave at the raft. That's enough for a small pod to explore. We could travel as far as dragons, maybe farther. Just think what we might find!"

Orm sighed. "We found a shark on our first journey here. What will we find next?"

CHAPTER 11: STORM PEARLS

Thunder rumbled through the dawn sky, on and on, like a symphony of dragon drummers. Arak slumbered on in his cozy shelter until a violent wind rattled the branches. He flinched in his sleep, startled awake, and stretched the sleep out of his body. He poked his head outside, filling his lungs with the cool, tasty air.

The storm finished with a shower of small ice-stones that bounced on the ground like over-active crickets. Arak collected several. He cut an ice-stone in half and studied the glassy rings. The ice ball was made from layers of lighter and darker ice.

It was like a fantastic pearl that Orm grew, when he changed the oyster's diet again and again. The pearl color changed with each diet change. Orm cut the pearl in half to show its rings of white, pink, violet and peach.

Pearls and ice-stones both grew in layers: one in the sea, one in the sky. Scree was right. Ice-stones were storm pearls.

These storm pearls were unusually round, like tiny

trance-stones. Arak stared into a cold crystal ball while questions crowded into his mind. How did trance-stones work? Why did each dragon use only one type of trance-stone? Could other stones work?

Arak grabbed a heavy bag, tucked away in a corner of his shelter. It held his collection of gemstone globes. He removed two and set them on the sand: turquoise and amethyst. Why had he never tried to use them as trance-stones?

Arak glanced at the protected cove, where the octopus guests would remain for another ten-day. He fiddled with his bag, thinking. Could an octopus communicate with a dragon using trance-mind? Could he keep in touch with his friends while they journeyed across the sea? Maybe they'd find an island filled with copper!

Arak had to know. But he was already called the Trance-Freak. His early, unexpected mind journeys had set him apart, and not in a good way.

When Arak was a dragonlet, he was often caught in a long trance. His mind was far away, questing. Once, other young dragons built a prison of heavy ice blocks around his still body. He returned to his body and awoke, numbed by the cold, alone in a cloudy-dim place. Arak thought he must have died. He struggled desperately to push his way out of the ice cage, scared and bruised and humiliated. He ran to his dam, still shaking, feeling rejected and hurt.

"Why?" he cried in anguish.

Arafine had wrapped her wings tightly around Arak, holding him in a warm, safe cocoon. She rocked her young son as gently as a summer breeze. "Because you have a gift," she said softly, "and they cannot understand."

"You entered the trance-mind with no training, before

you could fly. Your empty body just lay there for hours."
Arafine trembled. "I thought I would lose you. I still don't
know how you found your way back. It frightened the other
dragonlets."

She looked into his eyes. "You must learn to ignore or
avoid them. You see the world in new ways, and that is
good. Accept yourself. The seal of approval that truly
matters is your own."

She was right. Dragons didn't stretch their wings very
often. They didn't question what was or consider what
might be. The clan would think his experiments a waste of
time, useless dreams. But what was wrong with being a
dreamer? He just needed a safe, private place to
experiment.

Arak grasped his sack, looked out to sea, and launched
into the sky. Below, thin, scraggly bushes clung to a jumble
of offshore rocks. This barely qualified as an islet, but it
would do. He landed and tossed a few sharp stones aside,
clearing a smoother patch. Then he settled on the ground
and cleared his mind.

Arak focused on a crystal ball of clear, pale amethyst.
He stared into the globe until it seemed to shimmer,
glowing from within. Suddenly he was looking down on his
body from above. Trance-mind! He focused back into the
orb and returned to his body.

He reached for turquoise, cleared his mind, and
focused. Turquoise did not work. Next he tried a cloudy
moonstone ball with flickering blue lights. Success! Arak
worked his way through the stones. He tried one after
another, experimenting, oblivious to all else.

After he tried all the stones, Arak flew to the glacier.
He harvested a chunk of clear ice and made a globe using

125

dragon-fire. He meditated. Ice worked as a trance-stone. But an ice-stone made him crash!

Arak shuddered at that awful memory. His injuries from the crash were bad, but losing his trance-stone was even worse. Without the stone, he could not contact his clan for help. He expected a miserable death. Then Scree appeared.

What if no one had come? Would he have tried using ice for a trance-stone? Dragons believed that only one stone worked for each dragon. But many clear or cloudy stones worked for him, even storm pearls. The clan also thought only dragons could trance-mind. Was this wrong, too? Could he mind-speak with Scree?

A powerful wave of excitement grew inside him.

Arak flew to the shore and found Scree resting on a log seat, arms trailing loose in the gentle surf. He crouched at the edge of the sea and asked his question: "How did you calm your mind when you fought the squid?"

"I focused on a mental image, the bright star. I took deep, slow pulses of oxygen-water. I existed in the moment, letting go of the past and future. It's a skill I learned to focus on difficult healings."

Arak's inner wave of excitement became a towering tsunami. "Your mind-calm technique is the first step of the trance-mind!"

Scree turned bright apple-green. "Are you thinking octopi could do this?"

"I hope so. We think ice dragons couldn't talk mind-to-mind because they hadn't discovered this ability, just as they couldn't make fire. Maybe there was greater need for both when the dweer came. But the ability was always there, and it just needed training. Octopi might have this ability." The thought flashed through Arak's mind that dragons might owe the dweer more than they realized. Fire and trance-mind had changed the dragon world.

"I think Orm and Stur would want to try this. The trance-mind could be really helpful when we're skiff-flying."

Arak nodded agreement. "And perhaps you and I could communicate. Let's meet at the stream beyond the clinic. It's shaded by trees and hidden by bushes, so we can experiment in private. It's easier to learn without spectators."

The next afternoon, Arak sat on the stream bank with his sack of small gemstone balls. They were normally used to play a dragon game of marbles. Scree, Orm, and Stur each held a crystal ball in a coiled arm.

"To enter the mind-calm, focus on the mid-point of the ball," Arak said. "Put your mind into the sphere. When your consciousness leaves your body, it can only communicate with another trance-mind. Send a mind-picture. That should be easy for you, after concentrating to make your body-pictures."

The sky darkened into night as they tried the different stones. Stars blossomed overhead. Arak gave up on the transparent stones that worked for him, so they tried opaque orbs: black garnet, red jasper, turquoise and purple jade. But nothing worked.

Stur's arms drooped. "Perhaps we just don't have trance-mind ability."

Orm plucked three lustrous white pearls from his pouch. "We haven't tried pearls yet. You may need clarity, but what if we're drawn in by a shimmer?"

Each octopus concentrated on this new stone.

127

Scree's eyes glazed over and she slumped around her seat. Arak watched in tense silence.

Scree opened her eyes. Her entire body turned dragon-gold. "I looked down on myself! Just for a moment. What a strange feeling!"

Arak thumped his tail. "This can work!"

The following day, as the sun sank, Arak watched over a trio of limp bodies. Scree opened her eyes and her skin pulsed with colors. She seemed as excited as a dragonlet on an ice-slide. "We did it!"

Arak grinned. "I knew you could!"

Orm and Stur simply smiled, quietly relieved that this had worked. They had all exchanged thoughts.

The group practiced each day from afternoon to sunset. At the end of the fifth day, after Orm and Stur had left, Scree motioned to Arak. "Would you try the trance-mind with me?"

Arak nodded eagerly. He had worked hard, learning to form pictures in his own trance-mind, hoping this new ability would allow him to communicate with octopi. He entered the trance-mind and watched as a pale shimmer emerged from Scree. A night sky with glowing tunicate stars came unbidden to Arak. She had shared! He sent an image of Zarina's octopus snowflake. Then they each returned from trance.

Scree flashed a rapid rainbow of brilliant colors, one after another: ruby-red, topaz, emerald, turquoise, and amethyst.

Arak just grinned. He couldn't have said it better himself. He grabbed his silver flask, cooling in the stream, and poured two mugs of red-root tea. The rich, woodsy flavor was perfect for a celebration.

Scree sipped her drink. "We're charting new waters. This will really help when we're skiff-flying new waters!"

She lifted her mug to Arak. "To friends."

Arak raised his mug. "To kindred spirits."

He took another drink in a silent toast to an ice-stone, his storm pearl. So much had happened because of a storm pearl. His crash was a dark black cloud, but every cloud has a silver lining.

He would never have met Scree if he hadn't crashed. There would be no exotic trading festivals, no Orm to identify Arafine's mysterious illness, and no Scree to heal her. The devastating loss of his trance-stone had also driven him to experiment, finding success beyond the limits of clan beliefs.

There were layers within layers of silver linings amidst the cloudy gray rings of his storm pearl.

"We'll look for an island for your copper search," Scree said. "And now, you'll know what we find before we get back!"

* * *

Arak rustled his wings nervously. He dreaded the coming storm dance, and not because he feared lightning. He'd tossed bolts with Taron for many seasons and made more lightning casts than any other dragon. He loved flying storms. But this time Arak would be expected to choose a dragon-lady partner, and the only one he wanted had several suitors.

Clouds towered into the sky and darkened, but wind was minimal. It would be a perfect storm.

Most of the clan had already chosen partners. By tradition, the mated pairs flew up into the clouds first, wingtips barely touching as they spiraled higher. Then other couples formed and joined them. Taron and Erinite, without a hint of hesitation, leapt gracefully together into the sky. Arak felt a rare pang of jealousy toward his good friend.

Arak checked the vials of metal powders in his pouch. Five were used for artistic displays, to color the lightning red, orange, yellow, blue or purple. These rainbow colors burned in the clouds, more beautiful than an aurora borealis.

But dragons did not paint with green sky-fire.

Arak had one precious vial of chromium powder. The bright, red-orange metal would change a lightning bolt to vivid green. This special bolt was only made for a dragon-lady. She could accept or toss it aside. If she accepted, they were mated for life.

Lightning began to spark in the clouds.

Arak fiddled with the chromium vial's stopper. He polished his scales once more. Then, wings held rigid to control his tremors, he walked toward Zarina. She was still on the ground.

Arak suffered unexpected agonies when Karoon landed right beside her. Arak's rival puffed up his chest, extended his gleaming claws, and smiled suavely. Clearly Karoon expected her to be his partner. Arak held his breath. Then Zarina shook her head and turned away. Karoon snapped his wings angrily and flew off. Arak breathed again. But was she waiting for him? Or someone else?

Another dragon-lord landed beside her, shining and confident.

This must be her partner. Arak couldn't watch. He turned blindly away and stumbled into the sky, pelted by rain, seeking the oblivion of dark, distant clouds.

CHAPTER 12: BUTTERFLIES

Scree watched pairs of young octopi twirling through the water above the newly raked sand. They had changed their arm skin to bright colors: orange, teal, yellow, red-violet, and more. They reminded her of butterflies, in a dance of color as unique as the dragon-flake. The swirling octopus arms matched the drumming pulse of pounded shells, and they sparkled.

Scree looked more closely at the youngsters. How could they sparkle? "Shell bands! They shine like dragon-scales," she said to Orm. "This new fashion is really quite beautiful."

Orm's apprentice, Mir, spun up into the sea. Her arms wrapped into a tight spiral. Then she spiraled slowly down, arms stretched wide, gleaming like a fantasy creature. Pearly discs of abalone shell were tied along each arm. The shell discs made a continuous, flexible line of silvery-blue that flashed brightly, accenting her movements.

Scree's eyes glowed as she watched the dancers. She

wove her arms in a sinuous pattern that matched the beat, and she could barely restrain herself from twirling. But Orm lay completely relaxed on the sand. He'd soon be busy training three more helpers to tend the shellfish farms, which had tripled in size to accommodate trade and travel needs.

"The dancers have added more twirling to show off the armbands." Scree looked at Orm hopefully. "We could join them."

Orm shook his head, an automatic dragon-like gesture for no. "I'll wait for the circle dance. But the armbands are beautiful. Abalone shells are as lovely as pearls, and bigger. I wonder if dragons would like them, and trade?"

A change in drum beat invited adults to join in the traditional, whirling circle dance.

Scree wove her way through the clusters of purple sea fans that edged the dance floor. This level field of sand had been cleared for dancing in a time before memory. She and Orm twined arms, becoming part of a huge circle. Three arms were behind each octopus, serving as anchor. Three arms were ahead, to twirl the dancers.

Eight dancers took their places inside the circle. They faced the outer ring. Each dancer gripped three arms with an octopus of the big outer circle. On the beat, they were flung to the next pod-mate in the circle. The dancers quickly released their former hold and grabbed three new arms. Boom. They were flung again, releasing and grabbing arms.

Boom-boom-boom. The beat grew faster. Dancers were flung again and again, twirling about the inside of the circle, spinning like tops. The drumming changed. Dancers melted into the outer circle and eight new octopi took their places.

Scree loved the flying sensation as she was whirled about, twirling in circles within the big ring. She released three arms and quickly grabbed three more.

The dance ended and Scree leaned happily against Orm. "I wish we could do that every day!"

"But this makes it more special," Orm said.

A group of older juveniles played a game of Mimic. One octopus shape-shifted and color-changed to become the most unusual creature he or she had seen. The others had to copy it perfectly. Scree watched as an octopus changed into a blue lobster, and the other octopi matched him. The seven lobsters looked real. It felt strange seeing them transform back into octopi.

"Let's check out that play-scape," Scree said. "The pod used eight trees of kelp-weed! My arms were cramping up from knotting stalks and leaves."

Tiny octopi chased each other through the elaborate play-scape. They squirted through a maze of rings and tunnels, rapidly changing directions, sometimes camouflaging to confuse the "it" octopus.

"That's a worthy game. Excellent practice for escaping from sharks," Orm said approvingly.

"Or for catching them," Scree replied, with a teasing look. "Orm, I've been thinking about giant squid. We need a better plan. I found shattered coral heads on a not-too-distant reef. Squid must have broken them to reach the lobsters below. They have moved beyond their old range, and I think we'll meet them again."

Orm blanched. "Giant squid. We must tell Spar."

She nodded agreement. "And Arak. He might have some good ideas."

133

Scree began tasting the feast through the water. Clams and crab claws were dressed with pounded seaweeds, releasing a tide of flavors. Sweet, succulent abalone meat was a rare treat, available because several large abalone shells had been harvested to make the dancers' shimmering armbands.

Dragon spices seasoned many dishes. Ground peppercorn was worked into the oyster meat, while cinnamon bark flavored a meaty salad of mussels and scallops. Scree loved best the mashed red-root tea, which octopi found curiously relaxing and stimulating.

The music stopped, followed by three strong beats that were felt by all. Scree and Orm headed for the low stone tables, which were made from hundreds of small rocks. The tables were covered with giant clamshell bowls full of food. Octopi gathered in lines, circling around the sumptuous buffet. Each octopus filled a large clam plate, and small circles of friends settled onto the sand.

Scree, Orm and their apprentices discussed their new crop of rare, medicinal seaweed. A large reef fish swam into view, with curved gray scales that were edged in pure gold. The fish glimmered like a sunlit stream with overlapping ripples.

"Orm, look." Scree pointed at the fish as it swept past them. "Those fish scales ripple just like the clinic stream where we practiced the trance-mind. Imagine that, learning a whole new way to communicate." She absently drew a design in the smooth sand. It was the octopus snowflake that Arak had shared mind-to-mind with her. "The clan hosted a terrific trading festival. I miss the dragon-fires and story-telling."

"But it's good to be home, and our own festival is

exceptional. Trading with dragons is changing what we eat, how we travel, even how we accessorize. Octopus arms gleam like dragon wings when they're covered with abalone," Orm said.

Scree took a closer look at her mate. "You're enjoying the changes!"

"Of course. Change can be good." Orm smiled. "And it's really spiced up our food. But I still have concerns about the skiff voyage. There are even bigger sharks than the one that attacked Tara. Also giant squid and fierce storms. Huge waves are barely noticed down here, but they could crush a small skiff."

Scree sighed. Why couldn't Orm just relax and enjoy this opportunity? "We can handle sharks. Giant squid are dangerous wherever they are, and they're just as likely to come here. As to storms, we could always pulse home. After all, we do live in the sea."

Orm stared into the distance. "That would be a long, hazardous journey through unfamiliar territory."

"Arak would say you're 'feeling butterflies.' Don't you want to come?" Scree asked wistfully.

Orm twined arms with his mate. "Yes, but we should be prepared."

Scree pulled him into a closer embrace. "We are," she said, reassuringly. "And I'm teaching trance-mind to the rest of our skiff-mates. That could be useful, too."

Scree tilted her head back, watching a purple-and-pink sea dancer. The colorful creature twisted through the water overhead, like a butterfly she'd seen onshore. She finished her meal and scrubbed her shell-plate clean with sand.

Scree smiled with satisfaction as Spar distributed bartered items to eager octopi. Trading had changed the pod. Travel was now acceptable, in groups.

The skiffs, tied securely to the raft above, were the best barter of all. She could hardly wait for their journey! They could discover new reefs with powerful healing plants. Arak hoped to find a copper-filled island. There would be exotic sea life and glorious nights beneath the stars.

Orm was just borrowing problems with his worries.

* * *

Scree boarded the first of eight skiffs on a mild spring evening. She raised the skiff-wing, caught the wind, and flew the sea. The wind held steady and strong. Scree trailed an arm in the water, feeling the unique taste and temperature of the currents. She flew as fast as a dragon, her eyes shining with pleasure.

Scree chased a glorious sunset and traveled on through the night, following the stars. The fungus-coated mast of her skiff glowed yellow in the darkness, like a ghost tree. Her small fleet looked like a wandering forest, slipping across the water, heading south-west.

A few hours past dawn, Scree raised a square, yellow signal flag. She dropped the skiff-wing and veered to a collision course with her pod-mates, slowing to a stop as they met. They fastened their skiffs into one large raft. Scree was ready to socialize after a night of skiff-flying alone. Later, during the heat of the day, they would sleep.

A swarm of large jellyfish drifted past, pulsing their cloudy-white umbrellas. Several mid-sized turtles swam among them, feasting on the mindless creatures. "I wonder how Tara is," Scree mused, nibbling on salty seaweed from her cache of journey food.

"She'll return when her shell needs to be enlarged," Orm replied, relaxing in the shade as he ate fresh clams.

A patch of sparkling water brushed against Orm's skiff and he leaned over the edge to investigate. A cluster of small, round balls twirled by, covered with iridescent rainbows. Comb-jellies. Rows of clear, glassy hairs broke the sunlight into colors.

"Scree, look! These creatures are exquisite!" Orm covered his body with rapidly changing flashes of color as he tried to mimic the comb-jellies.

Scree laughed with delight. "You look like a frantic, fractured rainbow!"

Orm cloaked himself in one large, solid, arching rainbow. "Is this more dignified?"

That evening, Scree flew her skiff before the cool night wind. A school of silvery-blue fish launched into the sky and glided through the air like dragons, before splashing back to the water. Scree felt the sea again and tasted bitter tree tannins. She turned green with excitement, eagerly scanning the star-lit horizon for land. Nothing was visible.

There was still no sight of land after two more nights of travel.

In the morning, as the sun rose, pale gray clouds filled the sky. They slowly turned a hypnotic shade of deep rose. Scree studied the vivid display with a worried frown. She had learned many weather signs from Arak, and a red morning sky often meant that a powerful storm was coming.

Scree signaled the pod to merge together and rest during the day. Tomorrow they would head for home. She tied her skiff next to Orm's and slipped an arm into the sea, tasting the distinctive land-water. Scree looked longingly toward the unseen shore.

Orm followed her gaze. "It would take a big river to

change the sea so far from shore, and a large land to hold such a river."

Scree nodded. "Arak and I shared trance-thoughts, and he's excited. This land must be bigger than an island, so there's a better chance of finding copper. I wish we could keep going and reach the shore."

She sighed wistfully. "It's the border between land and sea. Just imagine the beautiful reefs."

"All borders are interesting, full of change and possibilities," Orm said. "We skiff-fly along a border. The sea supports us, but the sky-wind moves us. Sea and sky, land and sea."

"Clan and pod," Scree chimed in, with a twinkle in her eyes.

"I suppose so," Orm agreed. "I want to see this new shore. We should travel again."

Her eyes grew wide. "I never thought you'd want to travel to faraway places."

Orm smiled back, his eyes bright with amusement. "Really? Well, at first, I came along to help you chase sharks. But the journey itself is more captivating than I could have ever imagined."

Scree rested through the afternoon as the sun slipped lower on the horizon. Near sunset she raised the yellow triangle flag, signaling the pod to turn back. She felt an odd tang in the moist air, a prickly flavor/touch like bottled lightning. The storm was near.

Scree kept a watchful eye on the sky as they headed for home. She hoped the storm would not find them.

CHAPTER 13: HIGH SEAS

Arak landed on the dragon shore. Spring flowers perfumed the air and crickets sang merrily. It felt good to be back after dragon-weeks of searching from shore to shore for copper. He flicked his tail with concern at the unhealthy orange color of a dragon. Their mine was almost empty, and the remaining ore was often poisoned with thallium. What would become of the clan?

Kragor's tail dragged. He looked ill, weighed down by the bad news that he must report. "Arafine, we reached the southern beaches. We found no copper, and there's nothing left to search."

Arak stepped forward. "There are other options. I've kept in touch with Scree. She found signs of a large new land beyond the sea, with big rivers. She tasted fresh land-water in the sea, but had to turn back before reaching it. We could find this land and search for copper."

"That's too far for us to fly," Kragor objected. His eyes grew wide. "How did you even reach them by mind?"

"I've extended my trance-mind range," Arak said, matter-of-factly. Then his words tumbled out like a river.

"Yes, it is far away. We need a skiff. Taron and I designed a skiff that will hold five dragons. We built a small model to experiment. The deck is above the water to keep us dry. The belly must be weighted or it tips over. We would fill the belly with worthless rocks here to make the skiff stable, and replace these rocks with copper from across the sea."

Arak paused to catch his breath. "We could travel with the pod when they set out again in two moons. Octopi know the currents and they could help us navigate. Scree can find her way home just by tasting the water with a trailing tentacle."

Kragor and Arafine regarded him silently, eyes opened wide in amazement. They must doubt him. Was he Dreamer even to them? "It's not just a silly dream! This could work!"

"No, it's not silly," Arafine replied in a calming voice.

Kragor looked Arak squarely in the eye. Dragon-lord to dragon-lord. "Who would you choose to crew your skiff? You seem to have thought of everything else."

"Skiff crew?" Arak was thrown off by their quick acceptance. He focused on Kragor's question. "Taron and myself, because we know the skiff. Rikor, to help organize the trip. And you, for your experience hunting copper."

Kragor gave a slow, satisfied smile. "I'd like that."

"And the fifth crew member?" Arafine prodded.

Arak clicked his claws together, considering. "We would benefit from the perspectives of a dragon-lady."

"What about Driana or Zarina? A healer could be useful," Arafine suggested.

Zarina. She had been rather cool to Arak ever since the storm dances. But why? At least she hadn't chosen a mate, yet. If only he had the courage to choose Zarina for the crew! But that would mean almost two moons of traveling together. He would make mistakes and probably drive her away forever.

Arak bottled up his feelings once more. "Driana would be a good choice."

* * *

A large crew of dragons worked busily on the skiff, which was nearly finished. Arak fastened the last plank to the deck. Spring flowers were gone, summer was near, and the copper mine was almost empty. But soon they would find a new land to search.

"Hope this works," an old dragon said. "The copper rations just aren't enough. My joints hurt."

"It's a poor gamble," Karoon grumbled. "Surely there's more copper in our own land! Searching at home would be closer, safer, faster and easier."

"We've searched," Kragor responded shortly. "Look around you. There are orange dragons everywhere. We must search elsewhere."

Arak nodded in silent agreement. Oysters had been added to their regular menu as a lesser source of copper and it still wasn't enough. Summer was upon them and their need was urgent.

But the dragon-skiff was perfect. Smooth wooden planks met seamlessly to create a strong skiff with clean lines. A tall mast reached high into the sky. Huge, silvery-white wings were stitched from fish skins and safely furled. Arak's eyes glowed with pride.

A new concern crept into Arak's thoughts. This was

his idea. The hopes of the clan now rested on his wings. He also felt responsible for the crew. They would travel far from shore, too far to fly home. Storms at sea could be unpredictable, and there were giant squid. He slumped with the weight of new worries.

Arak studied the sparkling sea, brimming with possibilities. He snapped his tail. There were always risks. But there must be copper somewhere, and this was their best chance to find it.

"Here," said Kragor, handing him another basket of dried fish.

Arak stowed it with the tubers, seaweed, nuts, spices, tea leaves, water, fishing spears, venom, and extra wood and rope for skiff repairs. "We have plenty of supplies. I spoke with Scree in trance. We'll meet the octopi at the first raft."

Kragor nodded. "We leave tomorrow."

"I'll see you at dawn," Arak replied. Then he headed for the nesting shore.

Arak flew through a golden spear, smiling as the light splashed over him. He headed for another. These bright shafts of light pierced the clouds that were gathering for a summer storm.

Arak landed on the shore near Zarina; he just had to see her before he left. They touched foreheads. "I'll be waiting for you in trance every evening," he said, wishing he could say more. But she was with the nesting dragons. Could he tell her how he felt, if she was alone?

Arak greeted the other dragons. He gazed curiously at the beautiful nests. It was a clan tradition to make a protective ceramic bowl for a dragon egg.

Suddenly, cold rain pelted down.

Arak joined the small group beneath a huge weather-shade canopy. The shelter was made from large fish skins that were sewn together and suspended on long poles.

"This is comfortably dry," he commented.

"And our precious eggs are protected," Erinite replied. She heated her ceramic nest bowl with a whiff of dragon-fire. Then she carefully turned the large egg, which was nestled in fine white sand. Her artistic nest was an unusual green-blue, made of clay from a distant river. The frothy rim design was covered with tiny white seed pearls.

Arak pointed to the rim. "Now I know why Taron wanted so many small pearls. This looks like frozen sea foam. Your whole nest seems to celebrate the sea!"

Erinite laughed. "Pearls are the new gemstone, ever since you met Scree. And I like the meaning. Because a pearl grows slowly, in layers, it should encourage deep understanding in our dragonlet."

Arak crouched down near Arafine's egg, wondering what his sibling would be like. A swirled pattern of reddish-brown spots covered the large, creamy egg. The nest bowl was made of red clay spun with shimmering gold threads. A large cut ruby sparkled below each gilded rim fold. The nest had a stunning design with a traditional clan stone.

Arak looked into the proud, worried eyes of his dam. "Rubies and gold. For Kragor?" He put a comforting wing about Arafine. "Don't worry, we'll be back almost before you know we've left."

Dawn came early. Kragor, Taron, Rikor, and Driana joined him on deck. Arak leaned against the railing, gazing at the dock as they prepared to leave. He felt so energized that he could light a cloud!

THE DRAGON DREAMER

Arak fastened his eyes on Zarina as she waved farewell from the dock. She would be his trance partner during the voyage, having practiced daily to learn to communicate over the distance. Why? Did she like him? Or was this just an interesting challenge?

The crew cast off and headed west. Waves grew larger as they flew, and their skiff rocked and leapt like a wild creature. Arak and Taron laughed at each other as they skipped bent-legged down the deck, veering from side to side as the skiff pitched in the waves. The salty spray tasted of adventure and freedom.

"Stand here!" Arak cried. The boat rolled from left to right and tilted from bow to stern, moving constantly. But while he stood in this one magical spot, he remained still; everything moved around him. It felt like being in the calm eye of a storm.

Arak gave his spot to Taron. He stood in the stillness, flicked his tail and grinned. Kragor, Rikor, and Driana each took a turn experiencing the still-spot.

The waves stretched longer as they flew further from shore. "This is perfect! The sea's calm and the wind's holding steady. I'll lash the tiller so we can eat together," Arak said.

Would their luck hold?

At sunset, Arak entered trance-mind. All the crew had extended their communication range, but Arak's long-distance thoughts were still the clearest. Zarina stood trance-watch on the shore. She was the only other dragon who could easily reach across this distance.

How is the journey (Zarina)
The skiff is making good time. All is well (Arak)
Arak quickly ended their trance-talk, since the journey

144

must continue. The night sky was a black sea that sparkled. "Time to steer by the stars," he said.

"May the star-fires guard us as they guard the ancestors," Taron replied.

According to dragon-lore, the stars were fires. Endless generations of ancestors lived in the cold, distant after-home of the night sky. Warmed by their eternal fires, they looked down upon their past world and future dragons.

Arak studied the tiny dragon-fires that lit the dark sky. He looked due north and found the still fire amidst the moving sparkles. This star was a constant beacon that did not move in the sky. It was an amazing, dependable guide to steer by.

"The wind's shifting," Arak said as he moved the tiller. Kragor adjusted the skiff-wing.

Later, a new pattern of stars lit the night sky. "These are your stars," Arak said. Taron and Rikor took charge of the skiff.

Arak curled up in a sheltered place in the bow. He was soothed by the motion of the flying skiff, the drumming of waves slapping against the hull, and the crisp smell of sea air. He slept soundly until Taron woke him shortly before sunrise.

Arak steered the skiff past the octopus signal raft at dawn. He snapped his tail happily. "We'll be there before the sun sets."

In late afternoon, Arak spotted the first log raft above the octopus village. He adjusted the skiff-wing and came about, heading into the wind, skillfully slowing to a standstill as they docked.

Octopi boiled up to the raft, eager to see the dragon skiff and meet the dragons. They were fairly fluent in the new sign language, but few had met a dragon. They wanted an opportunity to practice their skills.

Spar welcomed Arak and Taron with the less formal greeting of old friends. "You two really improved the pod skiffs," he signed approvingly.

Taron grinned. "Our new design is *much* faster."

"And there's a harness to lift octopi onto the dragon-skiff, so we can visit," Arak said.

Clan and pod shared a relaxed meal, with dragons on the raft and octopi on the log seats that protruded at sea-level. Arak nodded with satisfaction. Octopi flew underwater, dragons flew in the sky. Now they would fly together on the waves, along the border between sea and sky.

* * *

A ten-day into their journey, Arak guided the dragon-skiff over long, smooth waves. He was riding the sea, flying without wings. Warm afternoon sunlight slanted through the rigging, casting web-like shadows on the polished wood deck.

A few white clouds began to form in the sky. Would it storm? They could use the fresh rainwater.

Scree stretched and curled each of her many arms, relaxing as she floated in a large tub of seawater on the dragon-skiff. She imaged a light sequence on her skin. "This is the pattern for 'welcome'. It's much brighter on a squid, when they flash red and yellow lights."

Arak frowned, concentrating hard as he drew the light sequence on fish-skins. "This light-language is complicated."

"It was hard to learn Vorm's language. Lights are so different from body movements and gestures. Vorm spoke

146

of life in the dark abyss. Light means everything there, like guiding stars in an eternal night sky."

Arak inhaled the pungent aroma of oil-berry ink, which blended curiously with smells of dried fish and the sea. "We should use larger skins and make really clear pattern signs. We might need these if we meet a giant squid." He flexed his wings for balance as the skiff rocked. "Could you show me what Vorm looked like, in trance-mind pictures?"

Scree removed the pearl that she carried in an arm sucker, always ready for use as a trance-stone. She focused and slipped into trance.

Arak concentrated on his aquamarine globe. Then he was seeing through Scree's eyes as a monstrous squid tore apart her undersea village. Long, snaking tentacles crashed through the water. Homes were reduced to rubble. Two octopi were plucked up, shaken senseless and devoured. Then a third.

Suddenly, Scree plunged a spear into the beast and the nightmare collapsed. Vorm lay like a mountain across the sand, with long tentacles. Later, he flashed a "welcome" pattern of lights with a poetic rhythm. Finally, Vorm said "farewell" with dimming lights.

Arak returned to his body.

"You were braver than I realized," he said, shaken.

"It was your gift-spear and the venom that made my attack possible. But, even after what he did to our pod, I could not have killed Vorm. He was desperately hungry." Scree looked out to sea. "Vorm was truly of this world. He loved the currents of the sea more than we could ever love a possession. He was vibrant, wild, alive. I feared him, but I miss him."

Arak nodded. "I didn't really understand why you cared for Vorm after his attack. But what he did was natural, not vicious. Life requires death; we kill fish to survive. And the light language is beautiful."

Scree lapsed into stillness.

Arak stretched his cramped arms and flexed his claws. New clouds were springing up in the sky like mushrooms after a rain. Perhaps they would grow into rain clouds. Their supply of fresh water was low and the air was hot. Some cooling rain would be welcome, if it was a mild storm. Then Arak was lost in thought, watching the rhythm of the waves.

Large rafts of yellow-brown seaweed drifted by, catching along the side of the skiff before moving on. Arak netted a cluster and dropped it into a tub of seawater. Tiny round floats grew among the small, leathery leaves. He picked it up, looking for roots. It seemed to have no beginning and no end. The mass felt crunchy and springy in his claws.

Arak shook the seaweed and snapped his tail in surprise. Two miniature fish and a crab tumbled out. Then he shook out a shrimp. He stared at the creatures as they sought cover in the water.

"Taron, come and see this!"

The fish, shrimp and crab all had mottled brown-and-yellow patterns. They matched the seaweed. A small filefish flexed the tiny file on its head, prepared to do battle. The crab found a scrap of seaweed that had fallen into the tub and scrambled aboard, blending perfectly. The sea-dragon fish curled its long tail and rippled the small fin on its back.

Taron pointed. "How strange. This fish looks like a

piece of seaweed with eyes." The tiny sea-dragon had long, leaf-shaped skin flaps over its entire body.

"It looks like that fish near the dragon-shore," Arak said. "But our fish doesn't have skin like sea grass."

Kragor picked up a piece of seaweed and studied it. "These are the sky-floats from the legend of Sorm! Remember? From the spring festival stories? Orm has to see this!"

The pod skiffs were tied to the dragon skiff while everyone rested through the heat of the day. Kragor lifted his friend aboard and settled him in a tub. Orm carefully removed a small piece of the new plant. He felt the springy seaweed and broke a float open underwater, releasing a ball of sky. Orm flushed bright green with excitement. "The legendary sea-sky."

Scree observed from her adjacent basin. "A whole world lives in here. They must spend their entire lives in a seaweed raft, to match like this. We should release them so they can stay with their kind."

"You're right. But I wish I could show them to the dragons back home." Arak put the seaweed in the net, added all the creatures, and waited as they burrowed in. He dropped the entire mass overboard, onto another seaweed raft.

"You can show them with your mind pictures," Scree reminded. "Yours are quite vivid now, like living dreams."

Arak gratefully accepted a steaming mug of red-root tea from Driana. He glanced up as a brighter patch of light slid across the deck. Golden spears of light punctured a thick, snowy blanket of clouds. It would definitely rain.

A thundering wave of water hit the skiff. The giant manta ray leapt a dragon-length out of the sea before crashing down again. A wall of water rose around it. The dragon-skiff reacted like a storm-blown tree, pitching to and fro while everyone grabbed for support. The huge fish leapt four more times and then sank out of sight.

Kragor held on tight to the railing as the sea grew calm.

"I wonder why it did that."

"I wonder *how* it did that!" Orm said. "Imagine an octopus leaping out of the water."

Kragor roared with laughter at this unlikely image.

Orm finished his tea and bid farewell. While boarding his skiff, he tasted earthy land-water in the sea and signaled his discovery.

Arak thumped his tail with excitement. They were nearing the new land! The golden glow of the sun was muted by clouds as it sank lower in the sky. It was time to cast off and fly the seas, following the stars by night. The sea was calm, with long gentle swells, and the skiffs flew easily through the fading light.

It began to rain. Cold, silvery drops pelted the gray-green water, and each drop splashed back as a ring of silver droplets. The sea looked like a field of yellow-flowers gone to seed, with fragile silvery balls made of parachute seeds.

Arak admired the field of seaflowers. Octopi must enjoy this rain, too, when the cold drops struck sensitive arms and slid across their skin. Rain was not felt below the waves, in the uniform embrace of the sea.

Arak reached out with his magnetic sight to feel the coming storm. It would not be a dangerous ice storm. But the wind blew from more quadrants here than at home, and there was such an expanse of sea to feed the storm that he could not judge its strength. The magnetic lines sparkled more than usual, so there would be lightning.

Maybe it would be a short, sweet summer storm. He instructed the crew to tie everything down, just in case. Arak raised a square red warning flag for the octopi: Be prepared for storm. His tail flicked nervously. Could the skiff withstand a strong storm?

The clouds grew darker and darker.

Suddenly, the rainfall intensified into a true storm. Winds grabbed at the skiff-wings and seawaters leapt aboard. Lightning crackled across the sky, followed by deafening claps of thunder. Arak tied himself to the skiff, ready to pull himself back if washed overboard. The others followed his example. Each being had a sharp knife strapped to an arm in case the rope tangled.

Arak reefed the skiff-wings to shorten them as the wind grew stronger. He furled his own wings, too. It felt unnatural to keep his wings so tightly folded against his back, but he did not want to be blown overboard. He constantly adjusted the skiff-wing, fighting both wind and wave.

The waves grew larger, with treacherously deep troughs. Arak fought to head diagonally into the huge waves, his muscles straining until they burned. The skiff would flip and sink if it was caught broad-side. He thudded across gray hills in a jarring, uneven rhythm that knocked him off his feet again and again. He struggled upright each time, bruised, never releasing the skiff-wing ropes. The cold, relentless rain chilled him to the bone.

Arak took turns with Taron, the only other dragon who could skiff-fly in a storm. But the break was never long enough. Arak's arms were on fire, his body was frozen, and his mind was a fog of exhaustion.

Black clouds covered the moon and stars. There was utter darkness between the long, jagged lightning strikes that burned through the sky. With each blinding flash he could see the small pod skiffs wrestling mightily with wind and waves. They were falling behind. Then the rain poured down in cold gray sheets. In the next brilliant flash he saw only rain. Arak felt numb inside.

The skiffs had disappeared.

The storm continued through the night, and they flew alone in a curtain of rain.

A gray dawn came and the rain stopped, but the waves were fierce. Arak flew through the following day beneath dark clouds, battling walls of gray-green water that threatened to swamp or overturn the skiff. This was a true test of his skiff-flying prowess.

Clouds covered the sky. The dark gray day became a black night as they out-ran the storm. Arak's whole body trembled with exhaustion from fighting wind and waves, constantly adjusting the skiff-wings. With calmer seas, he could at last loosen the lines and rest.

He was too tired to eat.

Suddenly, the clouds shifted and stars lit the darkness. Arak snapped his tail. The star clusters were not where they should be. "We're too far south! How far off-course are we?" He scanned the empty sea. "Where are the pod skiffs?"

Kragor followed his gaze, eyes wide with alarm. He flexed his wings wide and snapped them, flying straight up into the sky. He hovered at the top of the tall mast, vaning his wings as he blew a thin stream of dragon-fire onto the candle wick. The large, wax-filled bowl immediately caught fire, making a yellow star against the night sky.

HIGH SEAS

Arak looked up hopefully at the beacon. Surely such a bright signal would attract the missing octopi.

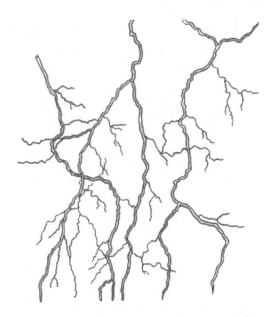

CHAPTER 14: BORN OF STORM

Arak breathed a sigh of relief. The fierce storm was over. He waited through the night, listening and watching for the missing octopi. Battered pod skiffs trickled in. Before dawn there were seven, including Scree's skiff that was already tied to the stern.

Orm was missing.

Arak flicked his tail worriedly. Where was Orm? Dawn bloomed, with a cheerful golden sky that did not reflect his mood. He doused the signal fire, which was useless by day.

Arak slipped into trance and traveled far, searching the sea for Orm. Although his trance-sight was blurry, he could easily see a pod-skiff. His mind wove back and forth above the sea, seeking. But he found no skiff. He came out of trance and squinted into the rising sun.

"It's light enough to search," Kragor said, staring out

to sea.

"I'm ready," Arak replied. Trance-sight was too blurry to see a few boards from a shattered skiff. It was time to fly.

Arak and Kragor flew a search pattern, traveling far from the dragon-skiff. They followed a reverse journey, seeking skiff debris or any sign of Orm. The day wore on, bleak and colorless in Arak's weary mind. His wings ached and he began to tremble. Growing increasingly desperate, he climbed higher in the sky, scanning the huge expanse of sea. But all he saw was the eternal sea. Spent, he and Kragor returned to the skiff.

"Where did you search?" Rikor asked.

"East. Maybe a current caught him. Try further south."

Rikor and Taron left to search.

Arak rested through the day, utterly exhausted. His muscles screamed from days of abuse. His mind had a hollow ache from too much questing and too much sorrow. He lay in the hot sun, which warmed his body but not his soul. He smelled roasted fish but had no appetite.

The searchers returned as the sun was setting, weary and worried, with no news to share. Scree entered the trance-mind and sought her mate. Her desolate eyes and grayed color clearly showed that there were no answering thoughts.

A large tree branch drifted past. Driana flew high into the coral-colored sky. "Land!" she cried.

Arak looked landward and sighed. The joy of success was marred by the agony of loss. He desperately wanted to wait, still hoping Orm would appear. But they needed to replace crucial supplies that were lost in the storm, and they *must* search for copper. He turned to Scree. "I'm truly sorry, but we can wait no longer."

Scree curled her arms in distress and nodded agreement.

The skiffs headed due west, reaching land just past sunrise. Scents of sun-warmed trees and foreign flowers blew around them, bringing memories of home. Arak anchored in a deep, protected cove. After dragon-weeks on the restless sea, sliding up and down waves, the stillness was a shock to his system. He felt disoriented, stumbling as he tried to walk across a deck that did not move.

Arak, Taron and Scree remained onboard to guard the skiff and watch for Orm. Octopi slipped undersea to explore. Three dragons flew ashore, ready to search from dawn to dusk for copper.

Arak spoke with Kragor every sunset, in trance. The explorers found pale blue turquoise in several streams, but no dark turquoise or copper nuggets. He could feel Kragor's bone-deep sorrow when he asked about Orm.

Arak came out of trance and drummed his claws nervously on the skiff railing, making an odd pattern in the dried salt. Three whole days of searching, and Kragor's group had found no hint of copper. He looked down at Scree as she once again came out of trance. Her eyes held an anguished look.

"Arak, Orm should have contacted me by now. He must be badly injured, or . . . dead."

"What about lost? That was quite a storm, and we're far off-course." Arak did not wish to consider a world without his brilliant, patient, quirkily humorous friend.

"No. I . . . ," Scree began. She suddenly froze.

A weathered board drifted into view, bearing a mottled, battered burden.

Scree bleached white and pointed. "Orm!"

Arak was instantly aloft. He hovered a second, remembering the injured dragonlet. His sharp claws would puncture Orm. He grasped the sodden board with his talons, struggling to lift both the board and Orm. Then he gently slipped the limp body into an octopus tub.

Scree reached across to her mate. He had a nasty gash across the back of his neck. One arm was half-missing, tied off with a rope, and the sensitive suckers on another arm were shredded. Scree ran her arm over Orm's lacerated neck, sensing, and trembled. "He's alive, but just barely. His pulse is very weak and he's in deep shock."

Arak handed Scree her healer bag, which had been lashed to the skiff for safe-keeping.

Scree crushed some red algae, rubbed it along Orm's neck, and dropped the rest into his tub. She massaged the base of Orm's neck and around the base of each arm, squeezing to help the flow of blood. She worked with an even rhythm, tirelessly, completely absorbed in her efforts.

Arak watched silently, daring to hope. If anyone could save Orm, it was Scree. He finally wrenched his gaze away from Orm and glanced toward shore. "Kragor needs to know." He took the trance-stone from his pouch and prepared to contact his sire.

Taron shaded his eyes against the slanting rays of sunset. "Look!" Fading light glinted off three golden spots in the sky.

Arak shook his head, bemused. "What amazing timing. Those two are truly connected."

Kragor landed and his eyes grew wide. "Am I dreaming?" His gaze swept the unreal scene. "He'll be all right?" He hesitantly reached out to touch Orm, but pulled his arm back. He shifted from foot to foot, full of nervous energy, eyes glued on his friend.

"I think so," Arak said, flicking his tail worriedly.

Driana fed Scree a nourishing meal while she worked without pause, continuing her impressive eight-armed circulation massage. Scree ate what was given without recognition, oblivious to all but Orm.

Arak turned to Driana. "Scree won't stop until Orm responds, but her arms are starting to droop. She needs help. I'm calling Stur." He banged two rocks together underwater with the signal for the healer apprentice: two quick hits, a pause, another hit. Stur came quickly and was lifted aboard into the third octopus tub.

"Can you do this circulation massage?" Driana asked Stur.

He watched closely. "Yes, and Scree is wearing out. I'll take over."

"No. I can do this," Scree insisted.

Stur touched her arm gently. "No. You're exhausted and your arms are beginning to cramp."

Scree searched his eyes and then nodded acceptance. Stur positioned his arms and Scree slipped hers off. He resumed her steady rhythm, continuing the massage that was Orm's only hope.

Two hours later, Orm's eyes fluttered open.

Kragor closed his eyes and went limp with relief, collapsing onto the deck. He had watched in tense silence for hours, unable to help and unwilling to leave.

Scree twined arms with Orm and looked deeply into his eyes. "Don't you ever do this again!"

"What? Don't get dragged across a reef? Or don't find my way home to you?"

"Orm," Scree replied, "always, *always* find your way home to me." They gazed at each other in a world apart.

Arak turned away, seeing too clearly what he wanted with Zarina. He asked Kragor, "Can I see what you've found?"

Kragor dug a clawfull of pale blue nuggets from his sack. "Low-quality turquoise, but there's some copper in this. We'll keep hunting. We caught a few big fish, too."

Arak hid his disappointment. Kragor's blue rocks were as light as a winter sky, so there couldn't be much copper. "We still have time to search," he said, trying to sound optimistic. The clan needed real copper.

Arak smelled the mingled aromas of spiced tea, crispy tubers, herbed greens, grilled fish, and a sweet-sour onion-berry sauce. There was even a tantalizing dessert of dried berries stewed with sweet-weed. He glanced at Orm and smiled. His friend was alive, and this was worth a celebration.

Arak leaned back against the railing, watching moon shadows slide across the deck while he ate one of the best meals of his life. Happiness flavored his food better than any spices. But there was one thing he simply had to know.

"Orm, how did you find us?"

"I followed the red-root trail."

Driana put down her mug. "The what?"

Scree shook with silent laughter. "When the storm struck, I feared the pod skiffs would be lost or destroyed. Whether lost or skiff-less, my pod-mates might survive. But we were off-course, and octopi would need a distinct trail to find us. We were drinking red-root tea, with its unique dragon taste, and the stash was out. So, I dribbled red-root into the sea as we skiff-flew, to flavor the water

159

and attract lost octopi. I'm afraid I've depleted your supply."

Kragor laughed, deeply and joyously. "I could not possibly imagine a better use for red root! Orm, welcome back! What happened to you?"

"I skimmed across leaping walls of water, seeking a safe passage. Suddenly, huge waves crashed into me from three sides. My skiff flipped over and was slammed into a reef. I was swept out, still tied to the rope. The skiff and I were dragged across sharp coral before I could cut myself free. I scavenged a skiff-board and floated, barely conscious, following the taste-trail."

Arak grinned, imagining a trail of tea. Now, if he could just find a copper trail! He stared into the dark forest beyond the moonlit shore. Tomorrow he would help with the search, and he was determined to find something better than that pale, almost worthless, rock.

* * *

Three long gray shadows rippled across the sandy beach, turning bright gold when the dragons flew over a large tide pool. Perfect reflections of Arak, Kragor and Rikor flew through the still water. They soared inland above the trees, seeking a good place to search for copper.

Kragor signaled and they landed in a clearing by a promising stream. "Look for turquoise or malachite," he reminded. Trace amounts of copper made the blue-green colors of these rocks, so they were indicators of possible copper veins.

Arak walked beside the stream, peering through the clear water, picking up rocks. Water served as a tireless miner, forever digging rocks from the banks. Mud and small stones were carried away by the current, but heavy metals like gold and copper sank to the bottom and stayed.

Arak flicked his tail irritably, tossing the rocks back. Nothing! Not even pale turquoise! His eyes were drawn to the dense forest that crowded close to the stream, dark and mysterious. Odd creatures scurried up huge tree trunks and leapt between branches. Silence fell where they passed. Nothing challenged the dragons.

"We'll try another stream," Kragor said.

They searched until sunset, seeking signs of the elusive copper. Then, still dragging empty sacks, they made camp. Tired and discouraged, Arak ate cold spiced fish and dried berries.

Rikor dumped a load of deadwood near the fire. "We haven't found copper, but there's no shortage of wood. I'll stand first watch."

The fragrant smoke brought a comforting scent of home. Wearily, Arak drifted off to sleep. He woke for third watch and quietly gathered supplies for breakfast. A hearty morning meal should give energy for a longer search.

Rikor woke at dawn, sniffing the air hungrily. He filled his bowl with steaming stew from the pot. "What's in this? Besides the cinnamon I smell?"

"Ground nuts, dried berries, and slivered roots from those fuzz-tail plants. They're everywhere," Arak replied.

Kragor tasted the stew. "Excellent. I was getting tired of fish."

They flew south and walked a new stream, searching. Soon each dragon had filled a sack with pale turquoise nuggets. It felt good to finally find *something*. But this was not copper, nor the real promise of a copper mine.

"Look!" Rikor reached for a large golden nugget, shining brightly among the dull gravel.

"They're beautiful," Arak agreed. "But not what we need." He tucked them away, with vague thoughts of making something for Zarina. Then he gathered more turquoise.

Kragor called a halt. They flew back to camp, deposited the bags of turquoise and headed for the next stream. The dragons searched stream after stream, sometimes finding pale turquoise but never any copper.

At dusk, Arak slipped into trance. He found Zarina's shimmer; she was waiting. Their trance-minds merged.

We found lots of pale turquoise, which may help, but no copper (Arak)

You found the land. I'm sure you'll find copper (Zarina)

Her comforting reply warmed Arak more than a steaming mug of hot tea.

Arak stayed in trance. He quested, his mind flying across the land, searching for a more promising area to hunt copper. Although his unique trance-sight was blurry, one thing was clear: this was not a good area for copper.

Arak slept uneasily and woke just before dawn. He flew very high above his questing region. There was a long stretch of curving coastline, a moss-like carpet of miniature trees, and thin silver ribbons of water. It was a bit like a map of the dragonlet world. And this area was not like the region around their copper mine back home.

They needed to change their search plans. But would the other dragons listen to him?

Two nights later Arak was back on the skiff, eating a fine dinner, drumming his claws nervously. He looked from dragon to dragon, trying to gather their attention. "I flew high to survey the land. Everything here looks much the same, with no obvious change in dominant rock type or formations. So we're likely to keep finding the same pale turquoise. We should raise anchor, sail along the coast, and start searching again in a new area. Then we'll have a better chance of finding copper."

Rikor shook his head. "We should complete the search here. It's best to be thorough. And this place has everything we need to re-stock the skiff: wood, fresh water, and food."

Driana nodded enthusiastically. "Huge red fish, potent herbs, and tasty tubers. We'll eat well on the trip home!"

Kragor tilted his head, considering. "Arak, you have a point. But we'd risk finding nothing at all if we move to another search site."

Arak gave his friend a "help me" look, but Taron just shrugged his wings.

"Our skiff is safe here. We might not find another good place to anchor."

Arak's tail slumped. They weren't willing to try another area, because they did not truly understand risk and reward. He was so tired of finding pale, pathetic turquoise. The clan would not be impressed.

Arak gazed into the mysterious, neglected forest and straightened his wings. He would seek other treasures. If they weren't likely to find copper, Arak was determined to at least find something special. He turned to Kragor. "Then we'll stay. But two dragons can search the streams just as well as three. Tomorrow I'll search the forest."

When the sun rose, Arak entered the forest alone. He stood in a cool, dark pool of shadow, listening, surrounded by odd rustlings and earthy scents. Huge, soaring trees made perpetual twilight on the forest floor. He breathed in the almost-familiar smells, trying to identify them, finding trees and flowers much like the ones back home.

Arak found a new type of mushroom that was creamy and hollow, with a delicate aroma. He ate the smallest sliver, testing. He smiled, savoring a delectable flavor that perfectly matched its smell. Then he waited, flicking his tail nervously. Mushrooms could be fatal.

Time passed, and he felt no dangerous numbing or tingling to indicate poison. He eagerly finished the mushroom. This would be a welcome treat! He hunted near rotting logs, gathering enough to fill three sacks.

A beam of light fell through a hole in the dense forest canopy, marking a path to the sky. He rose carefully through the small opening, wings tight, twisting up to the sun. Arak flew above the solid forest, skimming a vast sea of green swells, searching. He found a meadow that was bright with flowers and orange butterflies.

Arak basked in the warmth of pure sunlight, sniffing the fragrant air. He followed some fuzzy yellow-and-black insects back to a large, noisy tree. What was that strange, sweet smell? He reached into the hole, ignoring a horde of angry insects. The honey he found was liquid sunshine with a taste sweeter than red-berries.

Arak licked the golden sweetness off his sticky claws. He could never have imagined this treasure! He gathered honeycombs and flew back to the skiff, landing on the deck next to Orm.

"I'm healed. I want to explore," Orm pleaded to Scree.

Scree flushed red with exasperation and concern. "You almost died and you're still weak as a jellyfish. But if you weren't in this tub, you'd push yourself 'til you dropped."

Arak grinned, delighted that his friend felt well enough to argue. But Orm really should rest. Arak handed him a leathery leaf spread with honey. "Here, try this."

Orm tasted the golden treasure and wove his tattered arms enthusiastically while Arak studied him. A dragon would have died from such injuries. "Orm, you're amazing. You'll soon be as good as new. Even your arm will grow back. Dragons can repair a broken leg but we can't re-grow a lost limb."

Orm finished his tasty treat. "That's normal for us. What's really amazing is this honey. Still no copper?"

Arak turned empty claws to his friend. "Just pale turquoise, a poor copper substitute. Better than nothing, I suppose."

Orm twirled two arms in his thinking pattern. "I've never found the right seaweed to grow a copper crop for dragons, but there are new plants here."

Arak sat taller. "You've talked about this before. But how does it work?"

"All plants concentrate metals. Your almonds have boron, onions have selenium, and several seaweeds have iodine. We just need to find a plant that concentrates copper."

Arak frowned. "Would these plants grow the same metals in our seas at home?"

Orm nodded. "Seawater contains all metals, everywhere. The plant chooses what it wants. If seaweed concentrates copper here, it will also grow copper back home."

Arak exchanged a knowing smile with Scree: a project was the perfect way to distract Orm. And if he found a copper plant, that would be great for the clan and a success for this voyage.

The next day, Arak studied the pile of seaweeds near

165

Orm. The pod had collected an amazing variety: several leafy brown seaweeds, crunchy white seaweed stalks that looked like coral, a feathery red rope, a frilly purple plant, and seaweed with tiny green cups on delicate stems.

Orm chose another, comparing it with a pure copper nugget. He slumped in his tub. "I love the variety, but none of these will work." Wearily, he plucked up a piece of frilly, blue-green seaweed with purple streaks. He frowned in concentration as he tested it. Then he flushed green with delight. "This is it! It's rich in copper!"

Arak snapped his tail. "That's terrific! And just in time. We'll leave for home when the moon is full, in three sunsets." But Orm's reef was much deeper than this one. Would the copper-weed grow at home?

It was rather late when Arak sank into trance, but Zarina was waiting.

Orm found his copper-weed (Arak)

That's great news. Have you found anything new (Zarina)

Some beans I call cocoa. You'll like the hot drink. I've also found new herbs for your healing (Arak)

I'd love something new. Routine is boring. It makes the day last forever. Adventure must quicken the pace of life (Zarina)

You've become a philosopher (Arak)

Perhaps boredom is at the root of all philosophy (Zarina)

Arak looked forward to this time more than he cared to admit. He loved to hear Zarina in his mind, sharing thoughts.

Three days later, Arak stowed the last of the coiled rope on the skiff. He checked the barrels of water, collected from cold streams. Herbs and salted redfish fillets were still drying on racks. Zarina would love the healing herbs.

Taron helped tie down the cartons of dried seaweed, berries, onions, carrots, and tubers. "Driana was right. We'll eat well."

Arak sighed. "But we failed to find copper. How much will pale turquoise help the suffering dragons?"

Taron shrugged. "It will help. And you found delicious new world treats: creamy mushrooms, honey-roasted nuts and cocoa. Those beans make an amazing hot drink."

"I hope the copper crop grows well on a new reef," Arak said. A mesh sack filled with copper-weed was attached to each pod skiff, beneath the sea.

Silvery skiff-wings billowed into fullness as they caught the summer breeze. Arak glided out of the harbor, past a cluster of man-of-war. The iridescent, lilac balls sparkled like glass in the afternoon sunlight. Waves grew larger and shore-line trees shrank, growing smaller and smaller until they looked like moss.

Arak grinned when the skiff yawed around a wave, like a fish seeking its own way home. "It feels good to ride the waves again."

"And taste the salty spray," Taron added.

Arak sobered when the shore disappeared completely and the circle of sea closed in. There was a long, dangerous journey ahead. "But the sea is beautiful," he said softly.

A spectacular sunset was mirrored in the sea, with colors that ran through a rainbow of reds, corals, gold, and into the indigos of dusk. Clouds of tiny plankton flashed green when disturbed, marking their path. These glowing green trails followed the skiffs into the night.

* * *

Kelp fronds appeared on the waves and blinked out of existence as the skiff pitched down into a trough. Arak's eyes grew wide when he crested the next wave. Those were tree tops. He breathed deep, filling his lungs, savoring the faint scent of sun-warmed grasses. Land! Home, and Zarina. She was his contact, his anchor, the dragon he spoke to every evening. He willed the wind to strengthen as the waves flew beneath his feet.

The dragon shore grew steadily before Arak's eyes, sweeter than a river of honey. "We're home!" He turned the till, skillfully guiding the dragon-skiff to a soft landing at the wharf.

"It's been two moons since we left," Taron said, eyeing the shore hungrily. "My dragonlet will hatch soon." He tied the skiff securely to poles. The skiff would rise and fall with the tide, so he left slack in the rope.

It was late summer, but golden wings filled the sky like autumn leaves. The clan descended on the skiff. Arak shuddered at the unhealthy orange color of some dragons. They really needed copper. Orm's new seaweed showed promise, but it would be awhile before any could be harvested for copper.

Eager claws hefted the sacks of turquoise ballast. There was a small sample bag for each dragon with honey-roasted nuts.

A group of young dragon-lords gathered on the dock, muttering angrily.

"We worked from sunrise to sunset, day after day, building the skiff and gathering supplies. And this is all you've got? White turquoise?"

"We expected more than a lousy snack and cheap turquoise!"

Arak ground his teeth. "The turquoise is pale blue, but there's a lot of it. Try the food before you criticize it. And the next voyage should bring copper."

"What next voyage? Why should anyone help again?"

But one dragon did try the honey-roasted nuts, and soon the entire mob was distracted by this sticky-sweet snack.

Arak turned away. He re-checked the skiff, testing knots and stowing a few forgotten items. Then he stretched his wings and leapt ashore to join Taron and Kragor.

Arak stumbled when he tried to walk on land. A still surface felt unnatural.

The skiff had been in constant motion. For dragon-weeks he had walked with the sea, his knees loosely bent. As the skiff pitched from side to side he automatically veered left and then right. Arak matched the movements of the restless sea. He anticipated the rising deck with a raised foot. Now, he lifted a foot and nothing moved to meet it. He almost fell.

Taron laughed as he staggered onshore. "A hatchling walks better."

"Maybe we should fly," Arak said.

They flew to the sandy shore and landed near the nests.

Kragor immediately twined necks with his mate, so tightly that they were one.

Taron wrapped his wings around Erinite. Then he listened to their egg, and his beaming smile rivaled the bright moon.

"Welcome back, Arak," Zarina said. They touched foreheads.

Arak flicked his tail. Why such a formal greeting? Did she miss him at all? Karoon, of course, was close by.

Arak fingered a metal band in his pouch. He'd made the bright gold armband for Zarina during the long journey home. It was set with rare green garnets; the zigzag pattern of sparkling gems looked like emerald lightning. Would she want such a gift from him? They'd spoken almost every evening, but no emotion showed in trance-speech. Maybe he should wait a bit, to see how she felt about him. If he could tell.

Arak studied the artistic nest bowls. What was it like to build such a nest, following clan traditions? A dragon egg must hatch in a nest that combines land, water, fire and air. The First Dragon was born of these four elements, and all dragons since were born within them. A ceramic bowl was made of clay, softened by water, and hardened by fire and air to create an ancient magic that nurtured dragonlets, and a functional nest that held life-giving heat.

Two days later, Arak joined the clan gathering to witness the hatching of dragons. He took his place in the traditional loose, cloud-like circle of dragons about the nests. A continuous low thunder rolled from the large dragon drum, with an occasional crackling burst of lightning from metal plates crashing together. Dragons were born of storm.

Erinite's egg cracked first. "It's a dragon-lord!"

The piteous cries were surprisingly strong. Taron held a bowl of raw sturgeon roe, with a strong, fishy aroma. He eagerly fed the small, shining black eggs to his ravenous dragonlet.

"He has your appetite," Erinite joked to her mate.

Kragor stretched a long wing about his mate and pulled her close. "Arafine, your nest bowl is positively splendid."

"Just like your scales. I chose the colors to match you,

and rubies are said to make leaders." Their egg cracked in half and a miniature dragon-lady stepped out, unrolling her long neck and looking about imperiously.

Kragor crouched down for a closer look. "Well, the rubies were a good choice. She certainly looks like a leader."

Arak could see that his sire was already besotted with his beautiful new sister. It *was* miraculous to witness a dull, oval egg deliver a vibrant, shimmering dragon.

Zarina automatically checked the health of the hatchlings, and Arak sighed. She was always the healer. Now that so many dragons were sick, due to the copper crisis, she was usually at the clinic.

Arak fingered the arm band uncertainly. Zarina's life was filled with healing. Did she even want a mate? And did she want him?

CHAPTER 15: SQUID SIGN

The full autumn moon lent a pearly-gray glow to the sands. Scree waited at the edge of the village, curling her arms with worry. Dragons grew sicker by the day. Orm experimented with fertilizers, but the copper-weed barely survived. They must find copper on their next voyage.

Scree entered a light, calming trance and straightened the worry out of her arms. This was a time for celebrations. What would be would be. And then she'd fix it.

Moonlight faded away. Scree's arms began to dance with anticipation. Early dawn reached through the sea, bringing color to the gray reef.

A group of small octopi landed on the sand beside Scree and politely presented themselves, weaving their tiny arms to sign a greeting. The surviving octopi hatchlings had finally completed their instinctive migration home. They looked about, as curious as young dragonlets.

One juvenile seemed to be asking about giant squid. He stretched long like a squid and signed "big". The pod needed to know. And Arak. Scree would learn more after the feast.

"I wonder if any of them were born of our eggs," Scree said to Orm as he joined her. "A dragon would know."

"Of course. That's because dragons raise their own juveniles from the egg." Orm welcomed the first of the newcomers. They were perfect miniature octopi, each smaller than his head.

"I thought I might like that, if we only had one egg," Scree said. "Then I met Taron's dragonlet. He was so needy! I'd rather start with juveniles who can manage their own basic needs. Still, it seems harsh that so many of our hatchlings must die."

Orm twined arms with his mate. "It is sad. But these youngsters belong to us all. I remember feeling shy and uncertain, wondering what would happen next."

Scree gazed affectionately at Orm. "You've done well." She greeted another group. "I like to be here early to welcome them home. They've had a long journey."

These tiny octopi had struggled for survival since hatching, seeking food and avoiding predators. For each survivor, hundreds had perished. It was a brutal, lonely period in their lives. As they grew large enough to migrate home, the juveniles sometimes met other returning survivors. They banded together, growing in numbers, still vulnerable to attack. Now they were home and few would ever travel alone again.

Scree's eyes widened as another cluster of juveniles settled onto the sand. Another group! Why were there so many? "I wonder if the volcano had something to do with the amazing numbers. They keep coming!"

Orm looked puzzled. "The volcano? It's been almost two years since it erupted. You're right! These would be from eggs that hatched about two years ago, and . . . "

"The fish kills," they said together.

"The eruption killed fish, making hungry dweer attack dragons and a hungry squid attack us. But I never considered this possibility. With fewer fish to eat the octopi hatchlings, many more survived," Orm said.

"And then grew into juveniles as they migrated home. Everything is truly connected. Change one thing and you change the world." Scree laughed. "This should be interesting."

Spar's entire village turned out to welcome their newest members. As wave after wave of juveniles landed, the older members curled their arms in agitation. There had never been so many newcomers! Octopi lived in small, private caves that offered protection and a haven of solitude. Soon their caves would be crowded.

Stur said to Spar, "There are many natural caves under the second raft. We could start a new pod there."

Spar considered briefly. "Stur, that's an excellent idea. And you will lead the new pod."

Stur's eyes bulged with surprise. Then he smiled. "You're a master at delegating."

Spar chuckled. "It's the most important skill a leader can have."

Scree grabbed Orm's arm. "This new village could be perfect! It's less deep than here, more like the reef where we found copper-weed, so that crop might grow better. The dragons really need it." She turned dragon-gold and covered herself with scales. "The clan will be closer." She soared up and flipped back in a perfect arc, landing beside Orm. "And it will be interesting!"

Orm was less enthusiastic. "My farms and research are doing well here. It would take so much effort to start over. A Healer's bag is much more portable. But I'll think about this."

Several newcomers began flexing their tiny arms in agitation. They were copying the stress gestures of established pod members. Spar moved into the open space between the two groups of octopi.

Spar addressed the juveniles first. He lifted two front arms straight up and twined them together: "Be welcome to our pod." He gestured to a long table covered with seafood. "Eat."

The youngsters squirted eagerly toward the feast. As they crowded together, eating a meal symbolic of acceptance, their tiny arms relaxed. Abundant food was an unknown luxury, but acceptance into the relative safety of the village was an even greater treasure.

Scree tasted the spiced seafood through the water. "They won't expect those dragon spices."

"I expect them now." Orm twined arms with Scree. "Change can be good. We'll both move."

Spar turned to the older members. "We've been blessed with more newcomers than we expected. Each member must accept at least two. As they grow we'll need more caves, and there are many below the signal raft. Two moons from now, half our pod will move there. Stur will be the new pod leader, and I'll remain here."

A school of small fish appeared. Everyone watched the living river of silver as it swirled past, sparkling with random flashes as fish scales caught the light.

Spar continued. "This is a rare opportunity! We'll gain a new village, and each juvenile is a treasure of unknown potential. These youngsters were born of our eggs, and they have returned to us. Now, let's join them in the welcome feast!"

After the feast, adults and newcomers moved to the open dancing field. Some members simply chose two healthy-looking juveniles, content to rear whatever personality developed. Others sought specific traits. The youngsters melted away with their adult sponsors. Most pairs would develop a fondness for each other that lasted a lifetime. The bond between juvenile and adult octopus was often as close as that between dragon and dragonlet.

Scree surveyed the newcomers and found seven who gave better answers to her questions. She tested them with special games, seeking a quick mind and creativity. Then she headed for Stur and Spar with all seven youngsters in tow.

"Stur, you'll need a deputy leader and an assistant, and these two test well," Scree said.

Stur smiled fondly at Scree, his own mentor, the one who had chosen and cared for him. "Clearly, you know how to choose well," he joked, accepting the youngsters.

Scree turned to Spar. "And these are a good choice for you."

Spar twined arms with the tiny octopi, accepting and reassuring them. "I do need leader trainees, but why must you always surprise me?"

"To keep you on all eight toes." Scree turned dragon-gold and stretched tall, merrily tapping the tips of her "dragon-feet" arms on the sand. Then her color changed to a sober brown. "We need new leaders who are as steady as you. Squid are on the move."

A flurry of activity distracted Spar as youngsters were chosen.

Scree flowed slowly to her cave, still watching the choosing ground, matching the pace of her three small charges. A knot of juveniles remained on the open sand, not yet chosen, some nervously clutching the arms of journey-mates. Eight pod members rippled forward, together, and claimed them.

Scree had seen Spar ask these easy-going adults to wait until the end and work together, so that no youngster would face the uncertainty of being chosen last. Their leader wanted the new pod-mates to begin village life with dignity. Spar had hatched from a good egg.

Spar caught up with Scree. "What did you learn about squid?"

"They've discovered the juvenile migrations. Apparently giant squid are the new sharks, feasting on youngsters. And not so far away, either. I plan to track them down."

CHAPTER 16: CAVE PEARL

Sharp, icy snow bit into Arak's face. Dark clouds covered the mid-day sun as the rising storm howled. He needed to seek shelter. Instead, he stretched his wings and flew aloft one last time, feeling a reckless urge to challenge the wild wind.

Arak tumbled and twisted, rising above the storm. He straightened his body and surfed through the air, cupping his wings to catch the currents. It was glorious. This must be how squid felt in a strong sea current. Squid were deadly, but they knew how to enjoy life.

The storm grew and reached higher, nearly breaking his wings. He shortened them and carefully twisted his way down. Then he landed, folded his wings and bid the sky farewell.

Arak entered the dragon cave.

The close, shadowed spaces and dank, earthy odors almost overwhelmed him. He had lost the freedom of flight, but the shelter was undeniably beautiful. Rust, tan

CAVE PEARL

and white stone flowed across the floor. The cave was formed by water moving through limestone, carrying some stone away and depositing other. It was a living work of art, growing slowly over thousands of years.

Glow-worms covered the ceiling like stars in the night sky. These small worms lit the cave with a soft, yellow-green glow that gleamed off the water-slick rock. Arak loved best the tall stone columns that splashed down from the ceiling, like eternally frozen waterfalls.

A clear stream ran through the main chamber, connecting a series of quiet pools before it disappeared into a hole in the floor. Arak tapped the edge of the large central pool. A blind fish turned and swam slowly toward him, feeling its way with long, sensitive tendrils.

"Here you go," Arak said, tossing it a shrimp. The large fish snapped it up and wriggled with delight. It circled, clearly expecting more. This rare cave dweller was as white as the full moon, as white as an ice dragon.

Zarina glanced up from her work. "Last, as always," she said, sounding amused.

Arak walked carefully on the damp, slippery floor. "I prefer the outdoors. And the storm was perfect for squid-surfing."

"What?" Zarina gave him her full attention.

"Surfing the top of the storm, like this." Arak stretched tall and cupped his wings. "It's a wild ride. I felt like a squid caught in a strong sea current."

"Sounds dangerous, like the squid."

"Perhaps. I love their greeting." The wind howled, driving snow past the entrance. Arak noticed the sharp contrast between storm and cave. "Coming inside is like stepping back into fall. It's always the same coolness in

179

here. This thick rock is like a blanket; it works almost as well as the sea."

"So the sea is an octopus blanket. Well, these are for the clan. Help me spread the blankets."

Arak lifted a heavy stack. "Can't have too many." He remembered the fall warning signs: tree buds were thicker and the small brown dramurts were unusually plump, ready for a long hibernation. It would be a harsh winter. But the dragon cave was well-stocked with food, firewood and supplies.

Arak nodded. "Good workmanship. You made these yourself."

"How could you tell?"

"The flame-flower pattern. Have you found any new herbs for the clinic?"

Zarina shook her head. "I've been too busy, between the clinic and the blankets."

Arak grimaced. "I've been cutting fish into strips and salting them."

"Better that then skiff-flying," a dragon-lord growled, moving closer. "Wasting our time and supplies, giving us false hope. We should search here!"

"You can't expect instant success," Zarina protested.

The dragon turned to her and sneered, "Why not? He sounded so certain. We worked hard to make that ugly skiff. Useless dreamer."

Arak snapped his teeth angrily and stepped forward at the words "ugly skiff" and "dreamer". He stretched his wings wide and flexed his claws, ready to fight. He'd had all the insults he could handle. His eyes blazed. Nothing could make him back down.

The other dragon spread his wings, bared his teeth and

hissed menacingly.

Arak crouched, ready to leap, eager to finally fight back.

Zarina grabbed his arm. "No!"

Arak trembled with battle-rage and easily shook her off. Then he saw the pleading look in her eyes. He took a deep breath. A fight inside the cave could hurt others.

"Hiding behind a dragon-lady?"

Arak ground his teeth. This new insult was hard to take. "No. Zarina's right, this is not the place." He stepped back. "I'd fight outside, but our healers don't need any more dragons to patch up. And it doesn't really matter what you think. It matters what we find."

Arak turned away and walked deeper into the cave.

The blizzard soon filled the entrance with snow, blocking what little light there was. Arak carried load after load of firewood to the largest chamber, growing calmer as he worked. He and Taron built a big, crackling fire beneath a natural chimney hole in the cave. Most smoke escaped, but a pleasant woodsy aroma filled the chamber.

Zarina sat down on a natural limestone bench near the fire, waiting for the evening entertainment. Arak walked toward her just as Karoon strode forward and sat down beside her. He flicked his tail with frustration and turned away, but Zarina caught his eye and waved him forward. Arak sat on the other side of her.

"Thank you for backing down," she whispered.

"You were right." A fight would solve nothing, but only Zarina could have stopped him. His challenger had no idea how hard he and his skiff-mates had searched, or the dangers they faced. The clan desperately needed copper and, somehow, he would find it.

Driana walked to the other side of the fire, to the open floor between the fire and the wall. This cave wall was smooth and white, made of very fine, glittering crystals. It was a perfect background for shadows.

"This is the best part of being cave-bound," Arak said quietly to Zarina. He studiously ignored Karoon.

Driana raised her wings for attention. Then she used the firelight to make shadow-stories, creating elaborate vistas from the new world. She used claws, feet, even carefully positioned wings and a coiled tail. Dark and light wove together in life-like patterns. The dragon audience leaned forward, eager for stories of this distant land. Driana finished with the bee-tree and Arak's discovery of honey.

There were angry mutterings about copper amidst the applause.

Arak strode to the stage behind the fire. He faced his challenger, who was sitting right in the front row with a group of surly young dragon-lords. They were all drumming sharp claws on the bench and rolling their eyes in the most disrespectful way possible.

Arak took a deep breath and looked beyond the angry dragons to Zarina. He raised his wings.

"Dragons dance in thunderstorms. We seek shelter from ice-storms. This is the story of our sea storm." He swept his wings up to recreate the terrifying walls of living seawater. Shadow waves towered and crashed on the wall. A tiny dragon-skiff, made from his clawed fist, slid between towering waves.

Arak dropped a claw-full of sulfur powder into the fire at a crucial moment to mimic the explosive lightning. Boom! Boom! The dragons reared back, caught in the realism. The storm ended with Orm missing.

The surly dragons were sitting quietly erect, watching. Arak wanted to shout, "No. We weren't just sipping tea!" He sat back down, a bit closer to Zarina.

"That was quite a storm," Karoon said.

Arak could only nod, speechless with surprise. Was that a compliment? More likely, Karoon was just being polite in front of Zarina. Clever.

The next day, Arak sat alone on a cold cave bench, polishing his scales. He looked up and caught Zarina's eye as she walked by. "I'm beginning to appreciate what you said about boredom. Some adventure *would* quicken the pace of life."

Zarina laughed. "Stop polishing. You already reflect all the light in this cave. Let's play a game of stones."

The game room was in the next chamber. The stone benches were worn smooth by generations of dragons. These seats surrounded raised tables that were full of puzzles and games. A welcoming fire in the hearth gave an orange glow to the walls, and wavering black shadows. Arak smelled pine-scented smoke, roasted almonds, and earthy-damp limestone.

Dragons young and old chatted as they grew puzzle sculptures, jumped stones, or tried to out-guess an elaborate marble maze.

"Yesss! I win!" a dragon hissed, punching the air with his fist as he caught a ruby marble. An elderly dragon-lord nodded, and then dropped three bright gemstone marbles into the huge maze. The colorful balls clattered along rails of silver wire, dropping through holes, following unpredictable paths. Dragons bet on where each marble would exit the maze.

Arak stopped at a table with a pile of puzzle bags.

Each bag held many tens of carved onyx pieces, to make a shiny black sculpture. This was a challenge, since the bags held no guiding pictures. Would the lumpy black pieces connect to make a life-like dragon, a sturgeon fish, or a crab?

Arak studied a partly assembled sculpture. "Definitely a fish." He added two edge pieces. Then he glanced at a nearby table and stared.

"Puzzles are a useful distraction", Zarina said, picking through a jumble of black pieces between two sculptures. "Someone mixed these puzzle bags together. Now it's a real challenge!" She added a few more pieces. "Dragonlets start with simple flat ones. Assembling a sculpture helps us think in three dimensions, and that's useful when we fly." Zarina grinned triumphantly as she added the final wing piece to a gleaming black dragon.

Arak continued to stare at a detailed map of their land. The map was a dragons-eye view, neatly painted on a slab of white marble, with black lines for rivers. He noted the location of their copper mine and the curve of the coastline. He saw a flat dragonlet puzzle and something clicked. An idea sparked and then blazed like a lightning storm. This would really improve his copper plan!

"Arak, have you heard anything I said?" Zarina asked.

* * *

Arak crawled upstream through a dark, narrow, water-filled cave tunnel. He sipped foul air from the top of the ceiling. His body barely fit and he shivered beneath the frigid, black water. Soon he would grow too large for the tunnel. This was his last chance to search. If he didn't find copper, he might find a rare cave pearl for Orm's legend-stone collection.

Arak sputtered as he inhaled, choking on water. Then he found a small, precious pocket of stale air. Pointed, creamy-brown stalactites were barely visible in the pale glow of his fungus-staff. These cave teeth bit into his shins and gnawed at his tightly-folded wings, as if he was traveling through the mouth of a monstrous creature.

He had traveled since sun-up and his body was numb. His head hit a rock sill. Arak sucked air from a ceiling pocket. He filled his lungs. Then he dipped beneath the sill and squirmed through a long, airless water-way. The tunnel went on and on, completely filled with water. His lungs were bursting with need!

Arak thought he might drown here, alone, deep in the hidden passages of the cave.

Suddenly, the cramped tunnel met a large chamber. Arak lunged forward. He filled his lungs with the cool, wet air. He took another deep breath. Air had never tasted so good!

Arak reached into his chest pouch. He poured a sack of raw nuts into a rocky hollow and flamed. Then he slowly chewed the toasted almonds, savoring both the rich flavor and the warmth.

Thin beams of light fell from a few open shafts in the cave. The ceiling was a wonderland covered by rock straws; a shivering drop of water clung to each hollow tip. Arak lit a torch and the ceiling glittered like the dew-filled web of an impossible spider. So, this legendary place was real.

Arak had followed the cave's stream to its source because there might be copper. Nobody searched in such a difficult place, and no dragon had been here in generations. He had a search plan for the next skiff journey, but it would be far better to find copper now. He stretched his cold, cramped wings and flexed his claws. Then he climbed the smooth, water-slick limestone slope.

Arak looked diligently for signs of copper, checking first for greenish streaks in the flowstone. He explored small chambers and squeezed into tight, short tunnels. Nothing. In every way, this was a dead end. He flicked his tail in frustration and turned to leave.

Arak stopped and stared. A lacy veil of water splashed into a pool, echoing softly in the stone chamber. This was the pool of legends. Huge white marbles spun lazily beneath lime-rich drops of water. The pearls grew slowly with the cave, through generations of dragons, and few dragons ever saw one. He grasped a large, white sphere and stowed it in his pouch.

Orm would love the cave pearl!

Arak shook off his feelings of failure. Now he *knew* that the new land was their last best hope for copper. And he would find it, using his plan.

Arak gathered his courage. Then he plunged back into the cold, treacherous, water-filled tunnel. His hands and feet quickly became numb as he crawled along, disoriented, trying to breathe. He must return to the clan.

* * *

Arak took a seat near the fire, still shivering, waiting for the evening entertainment. Zarina brought him a steaming mug of tea and another blanket. "I thought you had more sense," she whispered sternly.

"I had to know," Arak replied quietly.

Erinite rose and walked to the fire, carrying a short wooden rod with holes. "Taron took a break from his endless skiff-carving to make this for me." She gave a

186

teasing smile to her mate and put the simple flute to her mouth.

Notes as crisp as a breaking icicle blended with the wavering sounds of winter waves cascading against the shore. These melodies were like ice-sculpture music. Then, adding a trill of rapid notes, she wove in the pattern of dragon-song. Taron joined her on a traditional dragon drum.

Arak sat still. This new, exotic blend of sound filled the cave like fragrant smoke. All the dragons were still, eyes gleaming in the firelight, listening. Arak smiled. Friendship with silent, underwater beings had sparked a series of inventions, and now there was a new type of music.

What would be next?

The storm finally broke during the night, as a dark new moon rose above a sea of snow. The silence felt alien after days of tearing, icy winds. Arak moved quietly to the entrance. Points of light from a trillion stars were reflected in the icy crust, sparkling across the snow with surprising brilliance. He stood alone, drinking in the bright, unearthly beauty.

The following dawn, he left the cave and entered a changed world. A thick blanket of snow hid rocks and bushes. Everything was clean and perfect.

Arak helped Kragor slide a huge block of ice to the sculpture circle. Then he worked on the benches.

"Arak!" Taron called. "Help us finish the ice slide."

"I was beginning to wonder if we'd have a Winter Festival this year," Arak said. He breathed flame along the lower part of the slide, melting the ice smooth. Taron worked near the top, finishing the steps.

Arak looked up and his eyes glowed. Zarina was in the clouds, hovering, holding still in the wind as she sculpted her snowflake. He fingered the gold armband, still in his pouch. Maybe after the next sea voyage . . .

He looked nervously out to sea. Squid were on the move. A giant squid was as large as the dragon-skiff, and could easily sink it. Scree worried about attacks and wanted to meet with squid to end the danger. Arak flicked his tail with concern. And the clan thought *he* was the dreamer! What if they met these giant squid on their voyage? He needed a solid plan to protect his skiff and his friend.

Arak sniffed the air, sorting the scents from the coming feast. The aromas blended together like perfect notes.

Taron flew down from the top of the slide. He landed beside Arak and cheerfully clouted him on the back. "There are some terrific new foods from our voyage!"

Arak nodded agreement. "But I wish we'd found copper."

"How's the copper-weed?" Taron asked, hopefully.

"Scree said it's not growing well."

An older dragon with orange scales tried to stretch his wings. He crumpled them back and hobbled on, unable to fly. Arak looked guiltily at his own golden scales. Young dragons were warned to keep their copper rations, to stay healthy.

Taron saw the dragon and shuddered. "He's been shorting himself, giving away his rations. We do need to find copper. But today, for the festival, let's just enjoy ourselves."

The cloud artists landed and carefully displayed their artwork on stretched claws. Zarina's crystal creation sparkled with a pattern of giant squid.

Arak took a closer look. "Terrific detail. I can almost see the squid-lights."

Zarina gave a satisfied smile. "Scree shared a mental image. I wanted the contrast of a powerful creature captured in a fragile flake."

Arak flicked his tail. If only it was that easy.

Zarina turned her snowflake to amber and hung it on the winter solstice tree. Then she, Arak and Taron joined Erinite within the circle of ice sculptures.

Arak studied Kragor's sculpture of their sea voyage. Visions appeared on the flickering sea inside the ice and vanished as the sun moved across the sky. As always, these images were extraordinary. But Kragor's sea moved. Three wave images surged, crested and crashed repeatedly. This was a new skill.

"You've out-done yourself," Arak told his sire, for once without a trace of jealousy. Art was Kragor's passion, and he was an amazing sculptor. Arak no longer felt a need to compare himself to his talented parents. He had his own passion for sea journeys and new languages. He could skiff-fly through a storm, trance-mind across the sea and read squid-lights. If he could just find copper, all would be well.

The sun sank lower and a man-of-war cluster appeared in the ice. It shimmered realistically on Kragor's sea. Arafine gasped. "That's just like my snowflake ornament! We still think alike." She twined necks enthusiastically with her mate.

Arak glanced at Zarina. She knew his fascination with squid. Did her squid-flake mean anything special?

Taron grinned happily as the dinner gong rang. "Smell that? It's New World foods."

"The clan saved most of it for this important meal," Arak said. "Zarina, I can't wait to try your new chocolate treats."

One long, stone table was covered with dishes of hot food: fish stew, grilled fish, smoked fish, honey-roasted almonds, salted pecans, crispy tubers, baked yams, sliced carrot crisps, steamed oysters with seaweed, hot cocoa, tea, and more. This table was warmed periodically by dragon-fire.

Another stone table was filled with cold dishes: fish eggs, fish rolls, spiced cherry clams, dilled pickles, dried berry compote, chocolate, the traditional snow pudding, and more delectable desserts.

Arak added a fillet of the tasty, red-fleshed fish to his plate, remembering the new world stream. That icy water was thick with huge red fish, leaping upstream. He grabbed a handful of honey-roasted nuts, savoring the smoky-sweet smell, feeling the warmth of the bright meadow where he found honey. He filled his mug with steaming hot cocoa and was back on the skiff, riding the waves, watching morning mist rise off the sea.

Erinite's eyes glazed over as she popped another chocolate-covered almond into her mouth. "Zarina, how *did* you create this chocolate? It's positively addictive."

Zarina ate a square of minty chocolate and sighed agreement. "Most of my experiments are not this tasty. I love the strong, deep flavor of Arak's hot cocoa. I wanted to make something sweet and chewy with the flavor of those beans." She smiled up at Arak. "Honey and cocoa beans are worth their weight in pearls."

Arak remembered the orange dragon. Pearls, maybe, he thought sadly. But these treats are not worth their weight in copper.

The following day, the wind picked up and the sky was overcast. Arak grabbed some fish rolls that were left over from the feast. "Taron, let's fly before the next winter storm drives us back into the cave."

"The meadow should be interesting," Taron said, as they both launched into the sky.

Arak skimmed just above the treetops, his toes cracking the ice from a few small, glassy twigs. "That flute of yours was inspired."

"It was really inspired by Erinite. She misses the ice music in the spring. I was working on our skiffs and thought, why not carve a music sculpture from wood? *That* wouldn't melt!"

"We mainly carve ice and stone," Arak said. "When did trees start growing here?"

Taron grinned. "I'm just glad they did. Our skiff wouldn't be the same without wood!"

The forest below was replaced by a white meadow with a twisting silver ribbon. They landed near the frozen stream, crunching through the icy snow. Arak made rings of frozen smoke with his breath. "Maybe we can catch some fish. This dried stuff's getting old."

Bubbles flowed under the thin ice, sometimes catching on thickened glassy swirls. A gray fish drifted slowly by in the dark water, barely visible beneath the reflecting ice. Arak smashed through the brittle surface and grasped the fish in his claws. He tossed it up onto the snow, where it flopped and grew still. Taron caught the next fish, and soon they had five-plus-three.

They walked upstream, throwing icicle spears at imaginary targets.

Arak stopped in his tracks. Six dweer were drinking from the stream. They lifted their snouts and snarled menacingly, displaying sharp, jagged teeth. All were gaunt and some had been flamed.

Arak knew he should fly away. Instead, he studied the starving beasts and remembered the well-stocked dragon cave. Scenes flashed through his mind: Dorali surrounded by a pack of dweer. A wounded dragonlet hidden by bandages. A field of dead dweer, frozen in unnatural positions.

Scree's words came unbidden to his mind. *Even after what he did to our pod, I could not kill Vorm. He was desperately hungry.*

Arak remembered his reply. *I had not really understood why you cared for Vorm, after his attack. But what he did was natural, not vicious; life requires death.*

Taron backed away. His eyes followed everything in the tense, uncertain silence. "Why don't we just fly off?"

Arak remained silent. His eyes were unfocused and he was as still as ice. At last, he picked up the sack of fish he'd dropped. He looked at Taron and instinctively signed his plan, still caught in his memories of Scree.

Taron lashed his tail sideways with surprise but nodded assent.

Arak took six fish from the sacks and placed them by the stream. He made the dragon sign for peace, folding his wings and crossing his front claws. Then he and Taron flew to a safe distance.

The dweer stared at them, backs still arched for battle. Fish smells filled the air. The dweer wrinkled their scaly noses and began to salivate. But they held still.

"They remember our spears and think the fish are

poisoned," Taron said.

Arak grabbed a fish. "Help me show that they're safe."

They took a bite from each fish. Arak and Taron placed them back on the snow bank and flew off, turning to watch from a safe distance.

The pack crossed the stream and sniffed the fish. Satisfied, each dweer grabbed a fish and moved apart, tearing into the flesh like the starving creatures they were.

"I would not have thought to try that," Taron said, as they landed back at the cave. "But Scree would be proud."

"Scree says that change has to start somewhere. We slaughtered the dweer. It wasn't really a battle because they couldn't fight back. They're still hungry because there aren't enough dagur to feed them. If dweer catch fish, maybe they won't attack dragons."

Taron grinned cheerfully. "At least we still have one fish each. But maybe we should only tell Arafine about the dweer. I'm not sure the clan would understand."

Arak looked Taron in the eyes. "Few would understand. I'm lucky to have you for a friend."

Tantalizing aromas swirled from the cave. "We're both lucky," Taron said. "I hope those tubers taste as good as they smell!"

CHAPTER 17: DANGEROUS DREAMS

A full moon lit the busy undersea village. Scree carefully detached glowing tunicate "stars" from the night sky in her cave, storing them in woven baskets. Orm would re-position his gift on her new ceiling. Then she filled sacks with her healer supplies.

As Scree packed her possessions, she recalled what Vorm had said. "We do not have caves like you. We live free in the water, and are not much burdened with things."

Her pile of belongings was now as tall as her cave. Scree pondered the wisdom of squid. What would it be like to have no possessions? Nothing to own or be owned by, surfing the sea.

Krees, Scrim and Tor rolled across the sand, trying to pin each other in a playful game.

"Do you still have your pearls?" Scree asked her youngsters. She had given them each a large white pearl for the New Moon Festival.

They stopped tumbling, straightened up, and nodded

solemnly.

Then Krees slapped Tor on his head. "You're it." She scampered away and the chase was on.

Scree smiled at their antics. She put her healer bag on the pile and went limp. Her arms lay in loose, random coils like seaweed washed ashore.

"Our experiences . . . our memories . . . all that we truly own is in our mind," Vorm had said. What a clean, tidy life. The temptation to simply abandon her mountain of possessions was surprisingly strong. But she needed her healer supplies.

Scree suddenly turned happy-green. Soon she would surf the sea, traveling far across the world, like squid. Dragons and octopi would journey together again. They might even see a swordfish! That huge, silver fish was a pod legend.

Orm poked his head in. "Are you ready?"

Scree grinned. "Always."

She rolled Vorm's huge pink pearl between two arms. This time they would explore further north, traveling through prime squid territory. Scree remembered Vorm's terrifying attack, but her eyes softened as she recalled their conversations. It was his dying wish to return the pearl to Veera. And she must meet with squid to protect the pod.

* * *

One moon later, Scree surveyed her new home with pleasure. It was below the second raft, much closer to shore. The water was less deep, so more light reached the sand and the plants flourished. Rings of tall, colorful seaweed made an elegant garden that hid her cave from predators.

Her healing supplies were properly stored. The

glowing tunicate stars were back on her ceiling. And, this village was within the reach of dragons.

Scree jetted to the raft and greeted Arak.

He grabbed a rock and flew down, using the stone anchor to speed his descent. Arak hovered above the sand, weightless in the water, and did a backwards flip. "So this is what it feels like to live under the sea." He followed Scree to her cave and peered inside at the glowing stars.

"What do you think?" she signed.

"Beautiful. It's a perfect night sky." Arak began to quiver and his eyes bulged. "Pod language is perfect for an airless world," he said. "But I'm not." He dropped the rock weight, shot to the surface, and climbed back onto the wood raft.

Scree followed, bringing a sack of seaweed. "The light is perfect here. Copper-weed grows in lush clusters. It's not copper, but I hope this helps."

Arak reached down and grabbed the large sack with both hands. He thumped his tail with enthusiasm. "We can really use this! There are so many sick dragons. We *must* find copper on our next voyage."

Scree nodded agreement. "We need to plan our squid excursion."

"We should scout for them during the next full moon," Arak said.

Scree drifted down to the sand. She was caught by the light current and pulled from side to side as she pulsed, moving in a pattern with the dancing water. Unlike their original village, the movements of the sea were felt here. But they were deep enough that storm waves barely affected them.

"Scree," Orm said, with a harried smile.

"How can I help?"

Orm gave her a large container of gooey oyster spat. "Spread this onto that boulder." He turned to direct another octopus. "Spread those clams evenly. We need to grow enough food for our next journey." He told a third helper, "These oysters are ready to culture black pearls."

Scree covered the boulder with oyster spat. The teensy oysters would soon fasten onto the rock and grow large. She glanced at her three fosterlings, who worked diligently nearby. "I've chosen well," she told them, smiling her praise. They twirled their tiny arms happily and continued seeding oysters to grow pearls.

"This was a good move," Orm told Scree happily. "Everything's growing well. The copper-weed needed this light. And the shellfish farms really benefit from these waves. They're flourishing."

Scree noticed that his arms were drooping. "Orm, you should rest. I'll take your youngsters. There's a pod problem and Stur asked me to look after his. Eight juveniles. I'll have my own pod!"

With Orm and Stur so busy, Scree watched their young octopi every day. Basic gestures were inborn, but most language and customs had to be learned. She taught the traditional pod language, skills, and more. Soon they could greet her in squid, dragon, turtle, or fish. Scree grinned. One did not need to be a pod leader to change a pod.

Scree's arms jerked as she felt the crash of the summoning stone. That should be Kragor. She and Orm squirted through the water to meet him at the signal raft above their village.

Kragor grasped a rock, plunged into the sea, and followed them. He poked his head into Orm's cave and

197

looked about. A glowing tapestry of red, green and blue tunicates covered the walls. "This is amazing!" he signed. Then he ran out of air and shot back to the surface.

Kragor dove again for another look at Orm's masterpiece. He exhaled slightly, releasing a stream of silvery bubbles that rose to the ceiling of the cave. The bubbles bumped together and popped, growing into a small, silver lake of air. The undersea air-lake had a mirror finish that caught the light. Kragor pointed and smiled.

Orm followed his gaze. "It's an underwater sky, like the legend of Sorm and his quest for sea-sky."

Kragor nodded. "Remember those glorious sunsets from our voyage, when the sky was reflected in the sea?"

"We were surrounded by color. It was like traveling inside a rainbow ball," Orm replied, his eyes bright with the memories.

"Sea and sky mix in interesting ways, like octopi and dragons," Scree added, laughing.

Kragor grinned. "Definitely!" He bowed farewell and flew back to the surface, leaving behind a trail of tiny bubbles.

Scree said to Orm, "I need you to take the pod of youngsters for the next few days."

"Why?"

Scree gave him a bright, mischievous smile. "I'll be hunting giant squid with Arak."

Orm blanched. "Whatever for? They're the hunters."

"It's time to change that. We need to know what they're up to."

"Scree, are you *sure* you weren't hatched by a dragon?"

* * *

Arak recognized the fearless light in Scree's eyes when they discussed giant squid. She wanted to confront them, and they could meet these deadly creatures during their next voyage. His new plan to find copper was not enough. Squid could destroy his skiff along with any copper he found.

Arak softened an empty honeycomb on a fire-warmed stone. He formed the wax into balls, putting the final touches on his own secret squid plan. Then he flew to the shore to check on festival preparations.

Arak landed just as Taron waded ashore, cold water sleeting off his scales like rain.

Taron pulled a long piece of seaweed off his ankle and announced triumphantly, "I finished the last octopus home!" His teeth were chattering.

Arak grinned. "Well done!" He eyed his shivering friend with concern and flamed a large pile of driftwood, which burst into a cheerful fire. Then he handed Taron three large, spiced fish rolls. "It's nippy tonight, and working in cold water really sucks the energy out of a dragon. Let's eat while you warm up by the fire."

Arak tossed two salt-soaked pinecones into the blaze, adding blue-green flames of celebration. He smiled with satisfaction. "We have enough caves for most of the pod. And a hoard of lightning casts, floats, tea, spices, glowing fungus lights, and skiffs to trade. Everything's ready!"

Winter stars winked overhead, and a cold wind blew. Taron moved closer to the fire. "We'll be leaving right after this festival. But it's so early, not even spring."

Arak nodded. "Our second voyage. We're truly desperate for copper."

At moonrise, Arak and a host of dragons welcomed the

199

octopi to their shore.

Trading began immediately. The pod arranged their items on the shore: sharp fish-fin needles, rare shells, pearls, colorful seaweed and vials of venom.

Scree gave Driana a large sack of copper-weed. "This is a gift. I hope it helps those sickly orange dragons."

"It will!" Driana eagerly plucked up five precious vials of venom, replacing each with a lightning cast. "With so many hurt dragons, I really need this venom. It's a stronger sedative than fire-weed."

Scree signed her satisfaction. "These lightning casts will protect our caves. The blue-ringed octopi were surprised by my interest in their venom. Now they're decorating their gardens with our pearls."

Arak showed a new pod skiff to a knot of octopi. "We improved the design, and there's a fish-skin shade over the stern. We also added a large container of red-root tea, for emergency sea trails. We can retro-fit your skiffs."

Arak bargained good-naturedly with Orm. He agreed to add these improvements to the skiffs, in exchange for a sack of pearls and a pot of oyster spat. Kragor wanted the spat to grow oysters near the shore, as food. Arak thought this was an excuse to spend more time in the sea near his glowing tunicate garden.

Kragor took a huge cave pearl from his pouch and, grinning, he handed it to Orm. "Here, for your collection."

Orm turned it about, staring in awe at the rare pearl. "I've never seen a cave pearl so big and so perfect. It's just like the Moon legend."

Kragor beamed with pleasure.

Arak smiled quietly. He had traded that cave pearl for Kragor's cave light balls, to use in his secret squid plan.

On the last night of the festival, dragons and octopi feasted on gourmet foods around a crackling dragon fire. The colored flames cast cheerful shadows.

Arafine raised her wings and conversations ceased. "We all love the foods from our first voyage, especially chocolate. Orm says it's a great source of iron. Now, Zarina will share her invention of our newest treat."

Two small sacks of roasted cocoa beans were passed around. Dragons inhaled the aroma and octopi felt the flavors. Zarina described her early attempts at mixing plant oils, honey, and powdered beans. She brought bite-sized samples of her latest creations: a chocolate bar made with ground nuts, and "chocolate snowballs" covered with delicate white seeds. Clan and pod cheerfully munched away on the treats.

Arafine led the applause. "That was a delicious story."

Zarina sat back down next to Arak in a quiet, shadow-lit zone beyond the fire.

Arak finished his chocolate snowball. "These would be perfect for the Winter Festival. How did you dream them up?" The fire crackled as a new log burst into flames with a bright shower of sparks.

Zarina smiled, but she flicked her tail worriedly. "I'm always at the clinic now, with so many sick and hurt dragons. My experiments are a great distraction for my patients, and they love eating my 'failures'."

Arak touched her shoulder reassuringly. "We should find copper on this next trip. We've planned much more time to explore."

Arafine raised her wings again. "Arak has a legend to share."

Arak picked up a sack and stepped forward. Dragons

settled back with rustling wings while octopi shifted on their seats. The fire crackled noisily into the silence, as Arak faced many pairs of glowing eyes.

Arak took out a large opal sphere and held it aloft, sparkling in the firelight. "This is a fire opal. It's rare, so not all have seen one." He reached into his pouch for five smaller opals. "Pass these around and experience the mystery." The opals were passed, with hushed exclamations at the hidden fire. Arak waited to recover the pieces. Then he raised his wings high, gathering their attention.

"The Moon and the Sun were in love, but they could not be together. The Sun was hot and came out during the day. The Moon was cool and came out at night."

Arak picked up a large globe of cool white marble in one hand and a ball of fiery orange carnelian in the other. He held them high, far apart.

"Once, the Moon decided to wait. As night ended she hid low in the sky. She was pale white, unseen against the white ice. She watched the fiery sunrise, awed by its beauty. As the Sun rose in the sky, the Moon rose after him."

Arak moved the spheres to follow the story.

"The Moon covered the Sun, holding him to her. The world saw the sky turn dark, as if night came early. The golden ridge scales of the Sun shone around her and this light was too bright to look upon. They were happy. But the Moon burned and the Sun grew cool. They could not stay together. Sadly, they moved apart. As they separated, a child of their joining fell from the sky. An opal was born, a cloudy moon with sunfire inside."

Arak held the moon and sun balls high, overlapped. He

moved the spheres apart, letting the hidden fire opal drop to the sand, sparkling as it fell. "It is as rare as their love."

Arak found himself gazing at Zarina as he finished.

Clan and pod enthusiastically showed their appreciation. Arak bowed and returned to his seat near Zarina.

"That was lovely," she whispered.

Arafine raised her wings for attention. "Scree has offered to share a legend that no other octopus or dragon has ever heard." Murmurs and motions of surprise rose from both land and sea sides of the fire.

Scree rippled quietly up the ramp to the shallow, water-filled platform. She raised two arms and silence fell over pod and clan. "This is the legend of Teera, the first squid. Vorm told me the story before he died."

"The Sun looked down upon the Sea. She was still and calm. No warm or cool streams moved through her. There was no life."

Scree paused, holding still in the relative silence, letting them imagine this lifeless world.

"The Sun wanted more. He cast a huge pink pearl into the cold depths of the Sea. The pearl was a warm and living stone. It warmed and changed the water. Currents flowed from the pearl. They were long, winding and strong."

Scree lifted Veera's pink pearl up high, turning so all could see. The lustrous surface winked with reflected sparks from the fire. The crowd whispered softly. Few had seen this rare pearl from the abyss, far larger than any from their realm.

"The Sun shone its red light on the Sea. The currents became solid arms. They were as flexible as a stream of the Sea, and moved like the flowing flames around the Sun.

The arms captured the Sun's light, sparkling with red and yellow. The pearl became a head, and two golden eyes flamed bright upon it.

"The Sun was pleased and named her Teera. She was a true child of the Sea and Sun, with arms like currents and flames. Her skin was dark and changing like the Sea. Her eyes and arms had golden lights like the Sun. She lived in the darkness of the Sea, in the abyss. But Teera spoke with the light of her father, the Sun. Life spoke with lights in the dark, secret places of the Sea. Currents flowed and twisted. The Sea had movement and life.

"Even today, squid live in the depths with their mother, the Sea. They surf her deep, strong currents. But when it is time to make new life, they rise to the surface and greet their father, the Sun. They feast on the swordfish, his gift. When new squid hatch they are pink, like the pearl, but they grow red like the setting Sun as they mature."

Scree bowed into the stillness. As if released, dragons vigorously flexed their wings and thumped their tails. Octopi flashed gold with appreciation and wove words of praise. Gold matched the dragons. It was now the accepted color for applause and questions at Trading Festivals. Several octopi added the diamond edges and texture of dragon scales.

Scree looked her surprise when Spar lifted two golden arms high and signed, "I never thought that they'd have legends."

"Squid are dangerous, but civilized in their own way. Their language is truly beautiful, with flashing patterns of red and yellow lights, and their words have poetic meanings." Scree made a series of bright spots on two raised arms. "This means 'greetings' or 'welcome', but it has a longer meaning: 'May you surf the tangled currents of the sea forever.' The literal translation is a window into another world, a different way of living and thinking."

"Do they make art?" Kragor asked.

"They tell stories and dance. They glow brightly through life. But they have no solid homes or possessions. There is no place for art. Giant squid mostly live alone. The Sea is their home, and it is everywhere. Vorm could not understand why a creature would seek the limits of a home that is tied to one place, or how anyone could be homeless. Home is where you are."

There were no more questions, so Scree returned to her log seat in the sea.

Arafine raised her wings for attention. "It's late, so we'll let the fire die out. Tomorrow, clan and pod will begin our second journey together. Honey and chocolate are delicious, and the copper crop is doing well under Orm's care." She bowed to him while dragons thumped their tails. "Let's wish this new voyage success."

Scree motioned to Arak. "Your opal has red and yellow flashes like squid lights."

"It does, doesn't it?" Arak placed the large fire opal securely in his chest pouch.

"We'll be traveling through squid territory," Scree reminded.

Arak nodded. "I'll bring plenty of fishing spears and you'll have the venom. We have skins painted with squid lights."

Zarina flicked her tail worriedly. "You really think you'll find giant squid?"

Arak shrugged his wings. "It's possible, but not likely. It's a big sea. We'll spend more time on land hunting copper."

Zarina grinned. "Don't forget chocolate!" She stretched her wings and pulled back, wincing in pain.

Arak stepped closer and saw for the first time an unhealthy orange tinge to her scales, almost masked by the amber firelight. He gripped her arms and stared fiercely into her eyes. "Don't short yourself, Zarina! I *will* find copper."

She gazed steadily back, making no effort to escape his grasp. "Arak . . ."

Whatever she might have said was lost when a young dragon with a network of scars landed right beside them. "Karoon broke his leg and you're best with that injury. He's at the clinic."

Arak released Zarina. She turned away and wrapped her wings affectionately around the messenger. "Tell Driana I'll be right there."

After the youngster left, Arak said, "She's the dragonlet attacked by dweer. She can fly. That's terrific! I haven't seen her around."

"Dorali is painfully aware of her scars. She spends most of her time at the clinic, helping, learning like a sponge."

Arak smiled at the image. "Sponges learn?"

Zarina snapped her tail irritably. "Dorali absorbs knowledge like a sponge soaks up water. She'll be a great healer, and having her around is almost like having my own dragonlet. Have a safe voyage!" She twined tentacle to claw with Scree and Orm. Then she touched foreheads with Arak, gave him a dazzling smile, and flew away.

Arak kicked the sand. This was just great. He was leaving, while his rival would be under Zarina's care. And was she even interested in a mate? The clinic was her home, and it seemed that Dorali satisfied Zarina's dragonlet interest. But worse, she was shorting herself, probably giving her patients part of her copper rations.

He kicked the sand again.

Arak looked up. Scree was watching him. He took a deep, calming breath. "Let's discuss the squid. What do you know of the abyss?"

*   *   *

The following dawn, Arak cast off from the dock. The skiffs flew due west, skipping across a calm sea before steady, moderate winds. Salt flavored the air and grew in crystal patterns on the mast.

Arak signaled the pod at noon. He furled the skiff-wing, slowing as the skiffs merged together into a raft. It was time to rest.

Kragor welcomed Orm aboard with a question. "How would you define art?"

"Art can be realistic or abstract, but it should be well-balanced. It must be pleasing to the eye or ear."

Arak finished coiling a long rope and stowed it safely. "What about taste? Zarina's chocolate snowballs are incredible."

Orm sighed and covered his body with puffed snowballs. "True. I made a sculpture that combines touch and taste." He described the special carving he'd made for Scree.

Kragor nodded. "Dragons can't appreciate texture the way an octopus can. But we can sense the crisp, shifting folds of the magnetic field. It's like seeing and feeling combined. We follow magnetic lines to find our way."

The sound of clinking mugs announced that it was time

for tea. Driana filled her kettle with water. She added a claw-full of fragrant red-root tea, a stick of cinnamon, a sprinkling of nutmeg and a pinch of herbs. Then she breathed bright, hot flames onto the sturdy iron kettle. The old copper kettle had been ground up for supplements.

Orm stared into the flames. Arak closed his eyes to better focus on the delectable and reassuringly home-like scent of spiced tea.

Orm turned to Arak. "You can see magnetic lines? How does that work?"

Arak reached into his pouch. "I can show you the idea. See how the clear light breaks into colors when it goes through this crystal?" He held his quartz prism at the perfect angle, and a bright rainbow appeared on the skiff-wing. "Colors are hidden inside the light. This crystal lets us see them. The magnetic field flows around the world, and a dragon's inner eye can see it."

Orm made a playful rainbow appear on his skin. "How do you use this invisible field for art?"

Kragor held his hands like wings. "I once made a sculpture with carved lodestones, a mobile. I could close my eyes and see/feel the bright shadows in the magnetic field." His hands flexed and swooped. "My silver-gray ice dragon moved with the wind."

Orm decorated his body with silvery dragons that flew in spiral patterns. "I wish I could see that. I wonder what senses exist in other beings? What would their art be like?"

Rikor joined the discussion just as Driana brought them steaming mugs of tea. He took a long drink and smiled. "I call it art if I like it, and Driana has perfected the art of brewing red root tea."

Arak accepted a mug, laughing at Rikor's pithy

definition of art.

Ten days later they spied land. Arak flew so high that he disappeared into the sky. He rocketed back and landed, shivering from the thin, frigid air. He wore a satisfied smile. "Travel further north, to the next bay," he ordered.

They anchored in the bay.

Arak, Rikor and Driana flew ashore to search for copper. Huge black trees towered above them, covered by the pale green fuzz of opening buds. Ice was melting, streams were swollen, and smells of waking spring filled the air. They landed by a promising stream. There were fist-sized geodes, like tiny caves filled with sparkling quartz crystals. But there was no sign of copper. The next two streams held colorful agates in shades he had never seen in a rock, but still no copper.

"These agates are stunning," Driana said, pocketing a few. She broke one open to see the rainbow-colored rings. "They're like Orm's special layer pearl, only brighter."

Arak dropped another useless claw-full of stones. He flexed his weary claws and snapped his tail irritably. "There should be copper." What if his theory was wrong? He remembered Zarina's amber scales and shuddered. He would find copper even if he had to search a thousand streams!

Slanting afternoon sunlight gilded the trees, glowing through glassy green leaves. Fanciful shadows shifted across the thick moss that carpeted the ground. This always seemed a magical time of day, when anything was possible. But it was late and Arak was too tired to scout again. "Here's a good clearing for our camp. We'll try again tomorrow."

At early dawn the dragon trio broke camp. They flew

high to scout from above and chose a new, more promising site. Lacy ferns clung to the banks of the stream. Their deep, blue-green color meant abundant minerals in the soil, and possibly copper.

Arak concentrated all his senses on his quest. He listened for the faint rippling of hidden streams. He felt for shifts in the magnetic field. He sniffed the air and tasted the water to detect any faint tang of copper. He scrutinized the banks and grabbed rocks from the stream bed, hunting greenish stones. After years of searching, Arak found copper.

"Rikor! Driana!"

They flew over to him.

"Copper!" Driana shouted, grabbing rocks from the stream and stuffing them into her bag.

Rikor thumped his tail. "And dark turquoise. Terrific!"

Arak moved on, concentrating, seeking the rich copper source. A cold spring burbled up through layers of rock and flowed into the stream. This water smelled faintly of copper. Arak dug into the stream bank and found no copper, but the scent was stronger. He saw the magnetic lines within the spring. He felt the current stretching far back, deep into the hill.

Arak followed the underground spring-stream into the hills, sensing the magnetic lines that snaked unpredictably beneath the ground. His legs began to shake. It was hard work, constantly skirting trees and leaping over brambles. The invisible, flowing lines were as twisted and slippery as an octopus' arms.

Arak felt a sun of energy and parted a tangle of vines.

Cool, dank air with a distinctive tang seeped out of the cave. Lumpy green walls stretched back into darkness. He

210

struck off a knob of rock. It gleamed like the most glorious sunrise. Copper! Arak snapped his wings and leapt into the sky. He spiraled higher, twirling with joy.

* * *

Arak landed on deck, flexing his wings for balance as he slid on the damp wood. He dug a claw-full of nuggets from his pouch. "Copper!"

Kragor hefted one of the heavy, greenish rocks and scratched it with a claw. It gleamed with pure copper. He thumped his tail. "Ruby-gold. Excellent quality! How did you find a source so quickly?"

"You know that game where we see who can fly the highest?"

"It's a favorite among young dragon-lords," Kragor said.

"It shows skill, endurance, and can impress the dragon-ladies," Rikor added, smiling at Driana.

She returned a sunny smile. "We expect it."

Arak juggled three copper nuggets. "It also shows an interesting view, like a map. The shore back home is almost the reverse of this shoreline. I thought about dragon puzzles and how pieces fit together. Our copper mines are near the shore where it bends out, and the matching shore here bends in."

Kragor nodded approvingly. "Puzzle piece shorelines. What a brilliant idea."

"So we searched that area first. There's plenty of quartz and agate near the bay. We looked further inland and found a stream full of turquoise and copper nuggets. There's a cave back in the hills with sea-green walls that gleam when scratched, the source. This should be a great copper mine!"

211

They celebrated with a feast. At night, strange glowing creatures rose from the depths. Three snake-like fish appeared with sharp, curved fangs and flashing pink lights. These black viper-fish chased a school of small copper fish covered in tiny blue lights. It was a window into the deep abyss, a world of night and light.

* * *

Arak felt the roll of the waves with satisfaction. They were five days into their return voyage, laden with honey and chocolate. But best of all, their hold was heavily weighted. It was completely filled with priceless ballast: copper nuggets and dark blue turquoise. There was enough to satisfy the clan through many dragon-hatchings.

Waves leapt brightly on the sea as if dancing to their success. Now, if they could just avoid storms. And giant squid. This was their mating season, when the monsters rose from the abyss.

Scree rested in a tub on the dragon-skiff. There was a far-off look in her eyes as she rolled Vorm's huge pink pearl between two arms. Arak eyed the pearl nervously. He knew what Scree must be thinking. How could she want to meet giant squid?

"It's late afternoon. Time to gather," Arak said. He raised a signal flag. Then he loosed the skiff-wing, using the tiller to turn as they slowed. The pod skiffs clustered together, forming one large raft near the big skiff.

"Scree, is this correct?" Arak asked. Two large fish skins with patterns of red and yellow dots lay drying on the deck. He dipped his brush into red paint, finishing the last of three light patterns for Vorm's name.

A large school of fish appeared, roiling the water. They were as lively and noisy as a boiling kettle of tea, leaping and churning frantically.

Then the sea erupted. A massive silver swordfish leapt gracefully from the sea, shedding a curtain of silver drops. It was nearly as long as the dragon skiff. The swordfish fell back into the sea with a thundering splash, ringed by walls of water.

Scree turned bright green and her eyes were huge. "A swordfish! Just like the legends!"

The swordfish tore through the school of bait fish, feeding on prey that was numbed by its sharp sword. Again and again the vibrant, metallic creature plowed through the ball of fish until few were left.

The huge fish flew into the sky again.

Suddenly, two clusters of coppery-brown snakes burst from the sea and grabbed for the swordfish. It desperately arced and twisted, ripping free from one of the giant squid. Dark wounds appeared on the side of the fish.

Scree shuddered. "No!"

The second squid was barely clinging to its prey, holding on by just two tentacles. The great fish rose and then fell on the squid, bashing it with all its might. But still the squid held on.

The swordfish leapt again, spiraling, trying to dislodge the heavy predator. The fish turned, slicing into the squid's head with its long, sharp bill. The gash narrowly missed a huge golden eye. The squid quivered and flushed gray. But it did not let go.

The fish leapt skyward once more, hampered by its burden. Dark stains ran down its side. Another tentacle fastened onto the gleaming scales. As the fish slowed, the first giant squid caught up. It flung a net of tentacles around the swordfish, dragging it under. The sea was eerily calm, as if the fierce battle had never taken place.

Scree sighed. "I know it's natural. I know the squid need this food. But it's hard to see such a beautiful creature killed."

"That was a huge fish. But those giant squid are as big as our skiff! Living nightmares!" Arak grabbed his paintbrush. "Let's finish these signs."

Suddenly, the silvery-clear water darkened to mud as an island rose beside them. The dragon-skiff rocked wildly. Dragons grabbed for anything solid to hold onto. Then, as the sea began to calm, a monstrous tentacle slipped over the side and shook the skiff violently.

Arak glanced at Scree. She had suctioned onto her tub, which was anchored to the deck. She flattened her body, camouflaged, and disappeared. A realistic pattern of tub boards ran through her body. Scree's color cells perfectly matched her surroundings.

Scree was invisible. Arak envied her talent, since this would be a great time to disappear. He held tight to the rigging as the skiff continued to pitch wildly.

Random items that had not been tied down flew overboard. Thank goodness the hold was so heavily weighted with rocks! The heavy ballast and deep keel gave the dragon skiff great stability and kept it from flipping over.

But the skiff could still be ripped apart. Nothing could withstand those powerful arms. This was Arak's nightmare made real. Octopi would be picked off and eaten. The precious load of copper would be lost. And the clan, including Zarina, would weaken and die.

Arak's body felt numb, but his mind was flying. The squid was even bigger than Scree's mind-images of Vorm!

Was it simply curious? It had never seen a skiff. Was this how it tested something new, or was it an attack? Was there a difference?

The other dragons snapped their wings in surprise and fear. Then Arak grabbed a spear. This was his plan. He leapt into the sky and hovered beyond tentacle range, his spear point aimed directly at the giant squid. The other dragons quickly followed his lead.

Fearsome, flying dragons must be a new sight for the squid. Afternoon sunlight gleamed off sharp copper claws, and the long spear points were as deadly as shark's teeth.

A huge, golden saucer eye emerged from the water and tracked the dragons. The squid released the skiff, which slowly resumed the gentler movements of the waves. But it did not leave.

Four dragons remained aloft. They threatened with their spears, circling beyond attack range but within the squid's field of vision.

Arak landed on the deck. The monstrous eye followed Arak and stared unblinking at him. This was the perfect opportunity to communicate with the squid. It respected the power of the spears and had just killed a huge fish, more food than it could possibly need. It might be their only chance.

Scree changed from camouflage to a solid, noticeable brown. She reached for the greeting skins and handed them to Arak. He held up the first skin, then the second and third in the light pattern sequence.

The squid's eye widened and its skin flushed red.

Scree grabbed two more skins, the ones with Veera's name pattern. "Try these."

Arak felt equal parts of fear and hope. This could

work. He held up the signs, one after the other. The monstrous eye blinked as if truly surprised. The squid flashed a return greeting, Vorm's name pattern, and what appeared to be a question.

Scree flushed with excitement. "She gave Vorm's name. I need more words!" Scree rippled up the side of the skiff, hung three arms over the edge, scrunched them together, and made light pattern sequences. Then she took the huge pink pearl, attached it to a long shaft, and offered her gift.

The squid removed the pink pearl and held it high in the fading light. She turned both eyes toward Scree and flashed a rapid, complicated sequence of yellow and red lights along her body. Scree blinked and shook her head. The patterns flashed too quickly to follow.

Kragor landed. "You gave it the pearl! Why do you think it's Veera?"

"She, not it," Scree corrected. "Vorm's mate. The only close relationship between squid is with a mate. Through many years, when squid gathered to mate, Vorm won Veera. Only Veera would ask about Vorm. She definitely recognized that pearl and responded to her name-sign."

Arak took the fire opal from his pouch, attached it to a spear shaft, and extended it to the squid.

Veera held the precious orb high, studying its random inner flames.

Arak knew that the flashing red sparks of light held no real pattern, no words. But the opal was as lovely as the pink pearl and probably new to Veera's realm. It was a unique gift that celebrated the language of the abyss.

Veera flashed another pattern of lights, more slowly.

That must be the squid thanks/acceptance pattern.

Scree imaged the squid greetings/welcome: "May you surf the tangled currents of the sea forever." Then she wove her arms in the octopus sign for "welcome".

Veera's golden eyes remained fixed on Scree. She moved her two front tentacles to copy the sign. The squid flashed more patterns and Scree responded. Then Veera jetted away to her new mate, who had surfaced with the dead fish and was watching from a distance. They flashed lights and dove deep.

Scree slipped back down onto the wet deck and climbed into the tub. She twined a tentacle with Arak's claws. "You acted quickly. And our language skins worked!"

Arak thumped his tail with relief. "Those giant squid appeared like a sea storm and vanished like a dangerous dream."

Kragor collapsed on the sodden deck. "That monster was more fearsome than I could have imagined."

Orm was lifted onto the skiff and he slid into a tub. "Introductions are too risky. I hope we've seen the last of them!"

Scree flashed red and yellow spots all along her body. "What? No more festive squid-lights?" She turned a sober brown. "We're lucky it was Veera. I fulfilled Vorm's last request. She was too surprised about his pearl to press the attack. And we communicated. That's a start, but nothing has been resolved. I'm still worried about our villages."

Arak picked up a broken mug and righted the teapot. "We certainly can't afford to lose the pod villages to an attack, or the copper-weed crop. What did Veera say?"

Scree slipped an arm over the side of her tub and tasted the tea washing across the deck. "It was hard to follow the

217

light-language, but I think she called you 'yellow sky swimmers'."

"I caught some of that. Maybe we'll become part of a squid legend. I'm glad she didn't stay for tea!" Arak flexed his wings for balance as the skiff rocked in a random swell. He gave Scree a searching look. "But what did Veera say at the end?"

Scree glanced sideways at Orm and nervously curled her arms. "She invited me to visit her realm."

Orm froze. His arms were stiff with concern. "And you politely declined?"

"It's a rare opportunity. How could I refuse? This skiff is at risk and all the copper. Both pods are at risk. It all started with the volcano that killed fish. Squid traveled further, hunting new food. They found the juvenile octopus migrations and will follow our young to our villages. Recently and in legend, giant squid attacked us in our homes. Must we cower and wait? We have never met them in their territory. This is the only way to end the threat, to make peace between our realms. And think what we could learn! Squid are masters of sea currents. They travel the world!"

Kragor flicked his tail rapidly. "This skiff, the pod villages and our copper-weed are all at risk. But what can one octopus accomplish? You would travel alone to an unknown place, surrounded by deadly creatures many times your size. Consider the danger!"

Arak crouched down to look Scree in the eye. "You do realize that this is not a sane venture? Even a dragon would think twice before such a journey."

"I've thought more than twice. But the potential benefits outweigh the risks," Scree replied firmly.

Arak nodded. Scree understood risk and reward. But he wished there was another way.

Orm gave a resigned sigh. "Scree, your love of adventure may overwhelm a rational fear of these deadly monsters. But you do know the squid better than anyone else, and perhaps this could work. When do you leave?"

"Tomorrow morning. And . . ."

"Can I help?" Orm asked.

Scree twined arms with her mate. "I was going to ask." She smiled at the surprise in his eyes. Then she straightened her arms and looked around. "This is dangerous but it must be done. I need your help, all of you."

Arak squared his wings and stepped forward. "I thought this might happen, and I have a plan . . ."

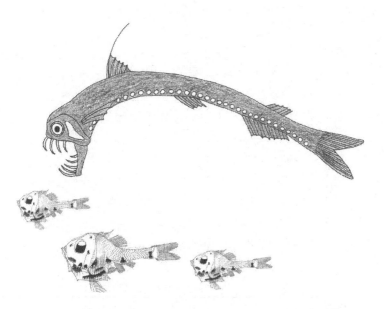

CHAPTER 18: THE DARK ABYSS

The following dawn, flaming gold clouds filled the sky. Scree waited on deck, ready to leave, holding no healer's bag. It felt as if she was missing an arm.

Orm's eyes widened with surprise. "Why not take your bag?"

"Squid are self-reliant. They don't burden themselves with stuff. Hoarders are seen as mindless gatherers, like lobsters that surround their dens with shiny rocks. A squid would only carry something as small as a single pearl. I must appear as a squid to be received as an equal. And I must be fearless."

"Well, if anyone can do that, it's you. But I'm glad you agree that bravery alone is not enough." Orm was careful not to touch the tips of her arms.

Scree felt Orm's concern through their farewell embrace, but he remained quietly supportive. "Thank you,

Orm, for understanding. You are my mate, and I will return to you."

Scree twined tentacle to claw with each dragon, last with Arak. He leaned down and touched foreheads, in a dragon-to-dragon manner. "I'll be waiting in the sky when you return," he said. His quiet belief warmed her more than a whole pot of red root tea.

Scree slipped down into the sea. She waited alone, holding only a short kelp rope.

The dragon-skiff rocked violently as a giant squid appeared. Veera flashed light spots to give her greeting, and Scree flashed color spots on her skin in response. Veera grabbed the end of Scree's rope. Scree gave one final wave before she was jerked beneath the waves.

The watery green light disappeared as Scree flew down through the sea. Blackness closed in and rows of jagged blue lights appeared. The glow of squid-light showed a school of small fish. With identical glowing patterns, these fish could easily find each other. This eternally dark realm was truly a world of light!

Scree finally touched down on flat, soft sand. She was surrounded by an odd kelp forest of swirling trees with flashing branches. Squid! It was still their season of gathering.

Veera flashed a brilliant light pattern and the forest grew still. She introduced Scree as "one-who-knew-Vorm". The squid asked questions and Veera repeated them slowly. Then Veera repeated Scree's skin-pattern replies, flashing brightly so all could see.

"Where do you live?"

"Below the yellow sky-swimmers, above the black abyss, in the realm of green light," Scree answered, as poetically vague as possible. Successful negotiations were not guaranteed, and she would not lead this fearsome horde to her village. Scree mentioned her dragon friends to subtly remind Veera of this powerful octopus ally.

The sand shuddered beneath forceful blows as two long, thick tentacles smashed down on either side of Scree. She looked up into golden eyes larger than her head. The monster gnashed its sharp beak, with loud snapping and grinding sounds. The menacing vibrations ran through her body like the barbs of sting-rays.

Veera's mate spoke with bright red lights: "How could a snack like you defeat Vorm? I challenge you."

The huge eyes stared into Scree. She did not need Veera to re-play the flashing lights. His message was clear. She was gripped by vivid memories of Vorm's attack, wrapped in powerful tentacles, expecting a gruesome death. These eyes were the same: intense, arrogant and angry.

Scree pushed beyond her fear. "I won like this."

She slapped an arm with a hidden needle onto each of the monstrous, threatening tentacles. The giant squid blinked. His hulking body convulsed. Both arms became numb, then seemingly dead. The secret venom was potent!

Scree quickly removed two small, wax-covered balls from her suckers. She scratched the surface to expose the sodium metal. Then she tossed the balls high into the water. They burned with a blinding, explosive light as the silvery metal reacted with water. Bright light was a fearsome weapon in the dark abyss.

The forest of squid retreated. The challenger withdrew, dragging his useless arms.

Scree flexed her arms. She turned in a slow circle, staring confidently at each squid while she quivered inside.

She still had six more venom balls and six sodium light balls. But she hoped she would not need them.

Scree's friends had worked through the night to prepare her secret defenses: wax balls with poison or light. Each wax ball fit perfectly into a sucker, hidden near the tip of an arm. Poison balls were made from sharp, hollow fish fin spines filled with venom, fitted into wax. Light balls were sodium metal covered with wax.

The venom and blindingly bright lights were unexpected weapons. The giant squid moved away from her. Only Veera stayed. Scree tasted fear through the water, an odd metallic flavor. Her show of force made her the equal of any squid. But she wanted a deeper, stronger relationship with mutual respect and understanding.

Scree said to Veera, "Your mate will recover. I chose not to kill. Vorm and I became friends because we had more to offer each other alive."

Scree emptied two eights of huge pearls from her middle suckers and presented them to Veera. Pearls were rare unless grown as a crop, so this cache must seem an extraordinary gift.

Veera warily accepted the gifts, clearly wondering what other unexpected resources Scree might possess. She stared at the shimmering stones, rolling them in a long tentacle.

Scree bowed respectfully to Veera and straightened her arms in a formal stance. "These shell-stones are a gift from our realm to yours. The black ones celebrate the dark abyss. The red-and-gold abalone stones remind us of your beautiful light language. You live free on the currents, but these can be easily carried with you, as friends-of-octopi."

Veera focused intently on Scree, and her huge body

quivered. What was the squid thinking? Scree wished she understood their body language.

"You are the first creature to learn our noble language, even though you lack our lights. It took courage to visit our realm," Veera said. But two of her tentacles gouged deep, angry furrows in the sand.

Veera did not seem pleased. Scree tried flattery. "Vorm spoke eloquently of your dances. Might I see one?"

Veera did not respond.

Veera's mate jetted forward, twirled once, and flashed lights. "I'm Tarm. There's more to you than it seems." He flexed a long tentacle. "My arms can feel again. Veera and I will dance."

Tarm spun and soared, flashing a rhythm of lights. Veera hesitated and then moved slowly forward to join his dance. They twirled side-by-side in tight, glowing circles, moving ever closer until they almost touched. Their arms meshed perfectly as they spun. Yellow lights flared at the tips and flowed upwards in unison. Red lights flashed another pattern, like drum beats.

Tarm and Veera swirled faster and faster until their lights blended together. Rings of spun light made one huge, glowing ball; they moved inside this. When they stopped, their long tentacles wrapped around each other in graceful curves.

Entranced, Scree automatically turned the brilliant dragon-gold that signaled appreciation. Then she spoke with the bright color spots of squid language: "Your dance was beyond beautiful."

Tarm released Veera and approached Scree. "Do octopi have dances?"

"We have several, but only one that is performed

alone: the pearl dance."

Scree removed a large white pearl from a sucker. She spun, swiftly flipping the pearl from arm to arm in graceful arcs. Then she quickened the pace. She had practiced to match the speed of squid, and soon the pearl was a blur. Her audience began flashing yellow lights in unison, to better see her dance. When Scree finished, they flashed the red lights of approval.

Tarm asked, "Would you join us for a feast?"

Scree smiled with pleasure, since this was a universal sign of acceptance. But still Veera said nothing.

Giant clams were brought forth, along with piles of crabs and fish. Although Scree had eaten well before leaving the surface, she was famished. The travels, Tarm's challenge, her dance, and the bitterly cold water all sapped her energy. Scree carefully followed their lead and tried everything, except for the fish.

Empty shells and fish skeletons were tossed aside, adding to the piles of litter that rimmed the gathering area. Hordes of small, ghostly white crabs boiled out of burrows and began cleaning the fish skeletons. The food scraps also attracted an incredible variety of glowing scavengers.

Scree feasted her eyes on the exotic life of the abyss. Most of the fish were black, and their shapes were amazing. The brilliant colors of the reef were found mainly in the beautiful lights of these colorless creatures.

Tarm settled his huge bulk onto the sand beside Scree. He flashed his lights slowly so that she could follow the words. "You danced well,"

"Thanks. You and Veera were amazing. Have you traveled far?"

"I've surfed beneath the ice at both ends of the sea.

The currents taste sweet under the melting mountains, and there are schools of small red shrimp as bright as sunset clouds. Huge white crabs patrol the sands." Tarm paused, as if considering something. "I've seen sky-swimmers before."

"Where?"

"I was hunting ice fish, far to the north. They're big and cloudy-clear, like ice. When one of the fish jumped out of the water, a white creature grabbed it and swam back into the sky."

"Was it bigger than the yellow sky-swimmers?"

"Yes, much bigger."

Scree turned bright green with excitement. "This is good news." An ice dragon! They were creatures of legend.

More squid visited Scree, and she was beginning to feel comfortable within this circle of giants. But Veera flushed odd colors and flashed her lights randomly. Why did she behave so strangely? What did she want? Scree tried to be polite and focus on her visitors, but she was worried.

Nothing was truly resolved.

Scree pulled her thoughts back to her visitor. This squid was describing a place where warm bubbles rose from the deep sea floor. "The sand is as yellow as our lights. The currents taste odd, like water from a tiny volcano that never sleeps. There are big clam-like treats that grow on stalks, as long and thick as your arms."

An old, graying squid approached and spoke of an undersea cave. "It's huge, big enough to hold me. There are sparkling white crystals as long as my arms, from wall to wall, like a maze."

Scree almost lost herself in the stories. But she again

saw Veera, lurking in the darker shadows beyond her visitors. Scree could almost feel the crushing weight from the miles of frigid water that separated her from the safety of her floating cave. She swallowed her rising fear.

A very young squid told of his northern adventure. "I tasted melting ice in the seawater. It was the time when ice leaves the land and returns to the sea. So I stretched my arms long and straight, close together. And I waited. There was a tearing shock. An ice mountain hit the sea. I rode the thunder-wave! It was faster than the fastest currents of the abyss!" He flashed an intense pattern of red lights.

"What a great ride! Did you ever catch another thunder-wave?"

Veera slid into view. Scree curled her arms. What did she want?

The young squid said, "Yes. The next time I felt the ice tear apart, I made myself into a ball." He demonstrated, bending long arms up over his head and twining the tips. Huge golden eyes peered out through his sturdy cage of arms. He unwound and continued the story.

"When the ice mountain crashed, the wave rolled me along the top of the sea. I moved so fast that I bounced on the water, and it felt hard. Everything blurred. It was great!"

The giant squid were surprisingly playful and eager to share their experiences. Scree wished she could travel to all of their adventure places.

At last, Veera joined her.

"Tarm is an interesting traveler. He sees life fully," Scree said, complimenting Veera's mate.

Veera flashed lights of agreement while she dug long, powerful tentacles through the sand. The trenches were

227

angry slashes deep enough to swallow Scree. Then Veera pulled herself tall, looming large. She towered over Scree. Twenty octopi tip-to-tip would not be this big!

Suddenly, Veera turned gray. She spoke with blinding lights: "What happened to Vorm?"

Her angry light-message was almost as bright as the sodium lights. Scree could not reply. She fought a powerful urge to flee. Would Veera risk Scree's poison, in the throes of her fierce rage?

Veera repeated her demand, with words as bright as lightning. "WHAT HAPPENED TO VORM?"

Scree forced herself to answer. "Vorm attacked me and I stopped him. He recovered. But Vorm was poisoned from eating my friend Tor. We became friends as he was dying. Vorm gave me the pink shell-stone, to return to you."

Veera moved even closer. Her massive bulk could squash Scree flatter than an oyster. "What did you do with his body?" Veera was watching carefully for the answer. Clearly it mattered.

Scree felt the poison-balls hidden in her suckers. If Veera gave in to her rage, would this be enough? "I helped my pod carry him to the edge. We released Vorm to the abyss. That was his wish."

Veera's color shocked back to its normal dark red-brown. "You honored our ways, even after his attack?"

"Yes." Scree finally relaxed her arms. She felt like a limp jellyfish inside.

"You are strange, but you understand honor. I will tell the squid what you did for Vorm. You are worthy of his friendship. His shell-stone is now yours."

Veera snaked a long tentacle to Scree, who formally accepted the huge pink pearl.

"Do you know what this represents?"

"It's like the stone that made Teera, the first squid. That's a beautiful legend of life and lights."

Veera's eyes widened, clearly surprised by Scree's understanding. "I gave Vorm this legend-stone when we first chose each other as mates. You sought peace between octopus and squid. You had the courage to face us, alone, in the abyss. This shell-stone is given back to you in peace. You are a friend-of-squid."

"May you surf the tangled currents of the sea forever," Scree replied, using the traditional squid salutation.

Veera settled next to Scree and answered questions about life in the abyss. Time flew by. At last, Scree stretched her cold, stiff arms. "I've truly enjoyed this visit. But my friends await my return, and I must leave."

Veera nodded understanding. "Will you miss the dark abyss?"

"The abyss is not truly dark. Life speaks with lights." Scree smiled as she quoted Vorm. "I'll never forget your beautiful dance. Thank you for the legend-stone."

Veera offered to tow her home, but Scree declined. She pulsed upwards, gaining speed as she rose. Soon she was flying up through the sea even faster than Veera had jetted down. Scree looked back. The squid were still watching, flashing bright lights that lit their wide-open saucer eyes. She caught one word: fast. They must be surprised by her speed.

Scree grinned with sheer delight as she rocketed toward the surface. There were four air bladders fastened below, where her arms met. They compressed to nothing in the abyss, so they didn't interfere with dancing. But when she rose through the water, the air expanded and they

229

pulled her along, flying ever faster. If things had gone badly, this was her escape plan. She moved faster than a hunting squid!

Now, would the lodestone work? It was late, and Orm would be worried.

* * *

Crystal lights blossomed in the night sky. Scree was late. Arak vaned his long wings as he flew search circles over the sea, trying to pick up her signal. It was well past sundown, their planned rendezvous. Had she survived her meeting with the horde of fearsome creatures? Even one giant squid was enough to make his toes curl.

The moon grew brighter as he flew, seeking the signal. Where was Scree?

Arak felt a minor shift in the magnetic field and veered west. The signal grew stronger. It must be the powerful magnetic lodestone that was attached to Scree. He was as sensitive to this force as octopi were to subtle tastes in sea currents. He could have sensed the lodestone many tens of dragon-lengths away. He pumped his wings, speeding to the source.

Scree shot up through the water and into the sky like a flying fish. She fell back to the sea and bobbed up and down with the waves, floating on the air bladders.

Arak shuddered as a powerful wave of relief tore through him. He twirled in the sky with fierce joy. She had survived!

He dropped a small kelp raft onto the sea, hovering while Scree dragged herself aboard and collapsed. Her body was gray and she seemed almost too drained to move. What had happened in the abyss? He grasped the tow-line and flew swiftly back to the dragon-skiff. The moon lit her face as she jolted across the waves. Scree's eyes were fastened on her beloved stars. She must have wondered if she would ever see them again.

They reached the skiff and Scree clung to the raft as Arak lifted it onto the deck. She slid into a tub, unrolled an arm, and held up the huge pink pearl. "Success! Our villages and the copper crops should be safe!"

Arak stared. Veera's pearl was as large as the icy storm pearl that caused him to crash and meet Scree. But this lustrous gift from the squid represented peace. Arak stood tall, with crisply folded wings. They'd all worked together and Scree had succeeded in this dangerous mission.

Orm flashed an unrestrained rainbow of vivid colors. He embraced Scree tightly, twining arms while careful of the toxic tips. "You became the peace envoy. And you did return!"

Scree gazed into his eyes. "Orm, I will always return to you." She gave him a dazzling smile. "The sodium balls you and Kragor made were perfect. They were spectacular in the dark abyss."

Orm smiled back. He did not let go of Scree. "We developed those balls as emergency lights for working in wet caves. I never expected to use them on squid."

Kragor nodded to Arak. "Very clever. I wondered why you were so interested in the light balls."

Arak shrugged his wings. "If life speaks with light in the abyss, then sodium screams. We had everything else we needed."

Scree laughed. "Arak, you even brought wax balls for the poison needles. I did need them. And the air bladders. I was too tired to pulse all the way back up. It's much easier to fly."

They shared a huge celebration meal. Scree lost her deathly gray color as she devoured clams and crab claws. She finished feeding and looked down with surprise at her mountain of empty shells. "I was hungrier than I knew. And this warm water feels so good! The abyss was as cold as ice."

Orm leaned forward eagerly. "What happened in the abyss?"

"I finally saw deepwater glowfish. I could not have dreamed up so many strange shapes! Some catch other fish by using a light they dangle in front of their mouth." Scree flashed fantastic pictures across her body. "I never saw such wicked teeth! It's a good thing the fish are so small. Most have blue lights on their bellies, like our reef glowfish."

Orm rolled his eyes. "No. The squid! What happened with the squid?"

All eyes were glued on Scree as she told her story.

Kragor shook his head in dismay. "How did you find the courage to face so many squid, all alone?"

"But I wasn't alone. I was filled with creative defenses from friends. With all of you helping, how could I fail? We're a perfect team. Kragor and Orm designed the sodium balls. Taron, Rikor and Driana helped make poison balls. Arak, your plan for the abyss worked beautifully!"

Arak straightened his wings with pride.

Scree grinned and covered her body in white dragon scales. "A squid saw an ice-dragon far to the north."

Arak snapped his tail excitedly. "I grew up with those legends, and always thought a trip north would be interesting. I even designed ice-armor for the dragon-skiff."

"Next summer might be an excellent time to hunt

legends," Scree said slyly, her arms dancing. She peered at her mate, who was as still as an iceberg. "Orm, what are you thinking?"

Orm sighed. Then his eyes brightened. "Scree, we all helped with the first skiff and then with your secret defenses. We *are* a perfect team." His eyes fixed on the distant horizon. "I just hope our next voyage has less excitement than squid visits!"

Arak followed Orm's gaze to the endless edge, where sea and sky met. He still traveled within a circle of sea and sky, but now he was also within a circle of friends. Arak surveyed his skiff with pride. The huge, silvery-white skiff-wing strained against the wind, gleaming like a flying ice-dragon in the moonlight. He flexed his wings, eagerly anticipating their northern journey.

Scree twirled beneath the stars. She studied the dark, mysterious border where starlight disappeared. What lay beyond? Her eyes gleamed. "I still enjoy traveling alone. But it's even better to explore as a team!"

She flashed squid-light patterns in a private message for Arak, since only he could read them. "You've come a long way from the ice floe, my friend. A dragon who can manage giant squid can do anything." A bolt of green lightning flew across her body and she smiled.

So Scree knew. Arak felt the golden armband in his pouch and smiled back.

CHAPTER 19: GREEN LIGHTNING

Lightning sparked in the clouds as the clan gathered for the storm dances. Arak nervously checked the vials of metal powder in his pouch that were used to paint sky-fire. One held chromium, a bright orange-red like the tips of dragon-lord scales. It would change a lightning bolt to a vivid green color like the tips of Zarina's golden scales. This special bolt was only for a dragon-lady, to accept or toss aside. If she accepted, they were mated for life.

Taron and Erinite flew gracefully up, wingtips barely touching as they spiraled higher. By custom, mated pairs were first to fly into the clouds. Then other couples formed and joined them.

Zarina was still on the ground, with Karoon and another preening suitor on either side of her. But she had not chosen.

Zarina was all things bright and beautiful, lightning come to life. She was also clever, talented, and had always accepted him as he was. She was the only dragon-lady that Arak had ever wanted.

He polished his scales once more. Then he approached, struggling to hold his voice steady. "Will you partner with me?"

She tilted her shapely head. A rare shaft of sunlight pierced the clouds and ran across her bright golden scales. Zarina was so lovely that Arak's heart almost stopped.

She smiled. "Yes."

Arak and Zarina leapt into the sky, flying higher and higher until they were above most of the lightning. Arak caught a small practice bolt and tossed it back and forth with Zarina before releasing it to the clouds. Then he flipped over and caught another lightning bolt between his legs, seeking to impress her. Not to be out-done, she furled her wings, twirled swiftly, and caught his throw.

Clouds all around were lit from within, glowing in colors like dragon-fires on the beach.

Arak and Zarina spiraled about each other, moving with the storm, concentrating to keep an exact distance between them like the experienced partners. They exchanged a rapid volley of lightning catches, challenging their skill with reckless abandon. The energy of the storm, the fireworks, and the dance surged through them.

A spectacular barrage of colored sky-fire lit Zarina; she glowed in rainbow hues. Arak ached with desire. He wanted Zarina to be his forever.

Arak trembled as he withdrew the special vial from his pouch. He had listened to her worries about becoming a healer. She had helped with his skiff designs, always confident that he would succeed. They were good friends. But were they more? Zarina had other suitors. She could still reject his proposal to be mated. They were so high up in the clouds, who would know if she refused? He would. She glowed like a rare golden pearl in the storm clouds, and in his heart. There was no other dragon-lady for him. He hesitated. But he had to try.

Arak caught a new bolt of lightning and twirled it rapidly on his copper claws. He poured in the red powder. A deep green color infused the glowing bolt. He saw her eyes widen. His heart beat faster.

Arak tossed the emerald lightning to Zarina.

*　*　*

"Catch!" Arak cried, tossing the skiff rope to Taron. They tied the dragon skiff securely to the dock.

This was their third voyage. Arak left right after the storm dance, urged to travel while the good weather held. After years of rationing and painful sickness, the clan just couldn't have too much copper.

"Welcome back, Arak!" Karoon shouted, clouting him roughly on the shoulder. No one called him Dreamer now. More dragons swarmed aboard, cheering loudly, eager to help unload the precious copper.

Arak blinked in surprise at the dragons' healthy golden scales. The bitter orange color was gone. "Taron, look! What a difference the copper has made in just twelve dragon-weeks."

Taron laughed. "Not just in dragon color, but in their attitude. I'm ready to stay home for a while."

Arak nodded agreement. "Can you take charge here?"

He flew to the shore and found Zarina, warming her nest bowl with dragon-fire. She looked up and smiled. She was like the summer sun, warming him with a glance.

Arak twined necks tightly with his mate. Then he

stepped back from the nest, drinking in the view like a thirsty dragon. They had exchanged mental pictures each evening during his long voyage, but she tantalizingly withheld images of her nest. He could only see that when he returned.

Arak studied Zarina's nest bowl, which was pale gray with a rim of ceramic lace. That lacy wave pattern must have been carved through wet clay before she hardened her bowl. Ten large black pearls gleamed around the top of the bowl. The large, speckled egg was nestled safely in a thick bed of clean white sand.

"I see you found a good use for those pearls I gave you."

"The best," she replied smugly, leaning against him. "You got back just in time. Listen, you can hear the dragon within."

Arak leaned down and listened carefully to the egg. "I wouldn't miss this hatching for anything." Then he stood tall and reached into his chest pouch. "Here, for my favorite storm dancer."

The bright gold armband was set with rare green garnets in a zigzag pattern, like emerald lightning. The gems glittered more brightly than diamonds. Zarina snapped her wings with pleasure. "I've never seen anything like this!" She slipped the band onto her upper left arm and squeezed the soft gold to tighten it.

"Orm described the gleaming abalone bands that pod dancers wear. Scree gave me a chunk of green garnet and I had gold nuggets. I wanted to make you something special."

Zarina cocked her head. "You made this on your first voyage, didn't you?"

"Yes."

"And then you waited. You took your time, but now you're mine."

Arak beamed and wrapped his long, golden wings about his mate, enfolding her in a tight embrace. "Yes, I am yours."

Zarina gave a sly smile and handed him a crystal ball, as clear as ice. "Here, for my favorite dragon dreamer."

Arak laughed. "Everything worth doing starts with a dream."

He held the trance-stone and felt a delicate carving, like winter frost. He took a closer look. A dragon wrapped from front to back around the ball, with its head and tail almost touching. Long dragon wings curled from side to side.

Arak locked eyes with Zarina. "It's an ice dragon!"

She grinned back. "And another dream."

Ice dragons. These legendary dragons still lived, and Zarina understood his need to find them. Arak gazed at her with such warmth that he could melt an iceberg.

GLOSSARY

Abalone – This tasty sea animal can grow to the size of two spread human hands. A big abalone shell can be thick. The inside is colorful mother-of-pearl, with overlapping layers of silvery pink, green and blue. (a-ba-lo-nee)

Bioluminescent – A plant or animal that glows in the dark, making its own light. Fireflies and many deep-sea creatures are bioluminescent. (bi-o-lu-mi-neh-sent)

Camouflage – An octopus can change its skin color to match, and hide within, its surroundings. This is an example of natural camouflage. (kam-ou-flaj)

Cloth-of-gold – This is real. The fabric is thin, strong, and woven from the wiry roots of the pen shell. It was once used to make beautiful gloves for ladies.

Dam – A dragon's mother. Arafine is Arak's dam.

Dagurs – These are not found in our world. Dagurs are tiny, primitive reptiles. They have short wings used for swimming, like penguins, and gold-brown scales. They eat sea-fish and are eaten by Dweer.

Dweer – These are only found in the world of the dragons. They are scaly, rust-colored, and eat dagurs. They are about the size of a wolf, and a hungry group can attack dragons.

Façade – An outer appearance that can be false. The dragons look fierce, but are usually good-natured. (fa-sod)

Famished – When you're very hungry. (fa-mishd)

Four-dimensional – We describe three dimensions as length, width and depth. Time is considered a fourth dimension.

A dragon artist carves many jewel facets into a huge block of ice. The sun shines through these facets to make glowing pictures in the ice that change with the angle of the sun. A sculpture that changes across time could be called four-dimensional.

Giant squid – These animals have eight long arms and two extra-long arms. Giant squid usually live in the deep ocean. They are intelligent, aggressive predators that can grow up to 43 feet long. Giant squid have huge eyes that can be almost 12 inches across. (skwid)

Incandescent – Bright, glowing, brilliant light or intelligence. (in-can-de-sent)

Inconspicuous – Someone or something that blends in and is not very noticeable, not attracting attention. (in-kon-spik-u-ous)

Iridescent – Shining with different colors, a sparkling rainbow effect. (ir-i-de-sent)

Juveniles – These are the young, immature members of a group of creatures. Puppies are juvenile dogs, children are juvenile humans, and dragonlets are juvenile dragons. (joo-ve-niles)

Limpet – This small, snail-like sea animal sticks tight to the rocks. It has a tent-like shell. (lim-pet)

Lodestone – This is a natural magnet. It's a naturally magnetic, iron-rich stone. (lode-stone)

GLOSSARY

Malachite – This beautiful gemstone has bands of light and dark green. This color comes from a tiny amount of copper. Turquoise is closely related to malachite, and is blue-green because of copper. (ma-la-kite)

Malicious – Mean, cruel, unkind, or intentionally evil. Karoon maliciously broke Arak's ice sculpture. (ma-li-shus)

Mesmerized – Amazed, fascinated, almost hypnotized by someone or something. Orm held the attention of his audience; they were mesmerized. (mez-mer-izd)

Mollified – Made more calm and satisfied, appeased, soothed. (mol-eh-fide)

Perpetual – Something that never ends. Eternal, forever. (per-pech-ooal)

Pithy – Concise, short, clever, amusing. Rikor gave a pithy definition of art. (pi-thee)

Quithra – This imaginary sea creature resembles a nudibranch, or sea slug. Slow, colorful creatures are often toxic and taste bitter; this is their defense. Medicines sometimes use the natural chemicals from bitter-tasting animals and plants. (kwi-thra)

Silver lining – "Every cloud has a silver lining" is an old saying. It means that even when bad things happen to you (the cloud), some good may come of it (the silver lining). Meeting Scree was the silver lining in Arak's crash.

Sinuous – A wavy, snake-like movement or form. Someone or something that moves in a graceful way, with curling, curving, or winding motions. (sin-u-ous)

Sire – A dragon's father. Kragor is Arak's sire.

Solstice – The winter solstice is the shortest day of the year; then days become longer. The summer solstice is the longest day of the year. (sol-stess)

Spawn – To release many small eggs into the water.

Sturgeon – This large, primitive, gray fish can grow to 12 feet long. Sturgeons are covered by hard, shiny, diamond-shaped scales. The females make thousands of oily eggs that are called roe, a tasty and valuable food. (stur-jun)

Tantalizing – Something that is tantalizing makes you want it, like the smell of a cake makes you want to eat it. (tan-ta-li-zing)

Tentacle – Flexible, boneless arm of an octopus or a squid, with strong, sensitive suckers to touch or hold. (ten-ta-kel)

Thallium – This extremely poisonous metal is right between mercury and lead in the chemical elements chart, and it is more toxic that both combined. Thallium has the chemical symbol Tl and atomic number 81. (tha-lee-um)

Tunicate – This small, soft, primitive sea animal often forms a group, or colony. Some types of tunicates attach to surfaces. They are sometimes called sea squirts. It is possible that some tunicates glow. (tu-ni-kat)

Vibrant – Someone or something that is very alive, or bright, or colorful. Vibrant is the opposite of dull, lifeless, colorless. (vi-brant)

Vivid – Strong, bright colors are vivid. A clear, detailed memory or description is vivid. (vi-vid)

Vindication – Arak was considered a failure for crashing. If the dragons could trade with Scree, this would vindicate him. Trade would justify his journey, a vindication that would make dragons think better of him. (vin-di-ka-shun)

Words can be beautiful and powerful:
"The pen is mightier than the sword(fish)."

In this snowflake, swordfish meet like
the dipping point of an inkwell pen.

AUTHOR'S NOTE

In Arak's world, dragons are large, lively, intelligent beings. They share shadow-legends, carve slides down glaciers, and grow fantasy snowflakes. Dragons love festivals, surfing the storm winds, and playing with colored lightning. The octopi are much smaller than dragons, very curious, and very clever.

Once, on a research cruise, I saw a deep-sea octopus. It was a rare creature, less than two feet long, with head and arms as clear as glass. The octopus' head was a bit smaller than mine. Its eyes were the same size as mine, a lovely yellow-gold color, and the black pupils were similar to mine. I looked into the eyes of the octopus and it gazed right back at me. This was truly an alien intelligence, and I wondered what the sea-being was thinking.

Most octopi can change their color, texture, and shape. Some types mimic other species, even shrimp, so realistically that people don't notice the difference. Octopi change colors to show emotion. They are very intelligent and have distinct personalities. It's not easy to judge such an alien intelligence, so octopi could be brilliant.

ABOUT THE AUTHOR

Jenny Burke has worked as an artist, chemist, teacher, and as a marine biologist, studying creatures of the dark abyss and diving on coral reefs. She lives in Athens, Georgia with her family.

Previously published books include **Crystal Geometry** and **Crystal Colors**. These hands-on math/science/art books have educational activities with crystals for people age six to adult. **Fantasy Snowflakes Activities** is a science/art book with dragon-grown snowflakes to create and color.

Visit Jenny at her website: **www.jennysburke.com**
Find recipes to make delicious dragon snacks!
Make deep-sea fish ornaments that glow in the dark.
Grow crystals as blue as the Hope Diamond.
Find her on Facebook: **www.facebook.com/jennyburke**

This snowflake is made of seals and kelp seaweed, because everyone needs a *seal of approval*.

Made in the USA
Lexington, KY
23 June 2016